—

1632 & Beyond Issue 3

Robert E. Waters, Bethanne Kim, Garrett W. Vance, Marc Tyrrell, Iver P. Cooper, 1632 and Beyond

Flint's Shards, Inc.

ERIC FLINT'S 1632 & BEYOND ISSUE #3

Editor-in-Chief Bjorn Hasseler
Editor and Webmaster Bethanne Kim
Editor Chuck Thompson
Cover Artwork by Garrett W. Vance
Art Director Garrett W. Vance

1. Science Fiction-Alternate History
2. Science Fiction-Time Travel

eBook ISBN: 978-1-962398-06-0
Paperback ISBN: 978-1-962398-07-7

Distributed by Flint's Shards Inc.
339 Heyward Street, #200
Columbia, SC 29201

Other 1632 Universe Publications

1632 by Eric Flint created the universe. Free download available at Baen.com/1632.html. All listed books available at Baen.com.

Short-List of Titles to Jump into the Series:

Ring of Fire anthology edited by Eric Flint

1633 by Eric Flint and David Weber

1634: The Baltic War by Eric Flint and David Weber

All books available through Baen.com, booksellers, and used bookstores.

Also Available:

Grantville Gazette Volumes 1 – 102, magazine edited by Eric Flint, Paula Goodlett, Walt Boyes, Bjorn Hasseler. Available on 1632Magazine.com.

1632 Universe novels and "Eric Flint, Ring of Fire Series" on Baen.com

Recently Released:

A Diogenes Club for the Czar by Gorg Huff and Paula Goodlett

Forthcoming:

February 6, 2024: *An Angel Called Peterbilt* by Eric Flint, Gorg Huff, and Paula Goodlett

Ongoing: Baen is re-releasing select 1632 books originally released by Eric Flint's Ring of Fire Press, starting with Bjorn Hasseler's NESS books. Please check the Baen.com e-arc bundles and new releases regularly!

Odd numbered months: New issues of Eric Flint's 1632 & Beyond

Key Storyline Points
by Bjorn Hasseler, Editor-in-Chief

T his section is both orientation and review for readers and writers. It necessarily contains spoilers. If you don't like spoilers, we recommend skipping to the next article or downloading a copy of *1632* from the Baen Free Library: https://www.baen.com/1632.html

Timeline

Sunday, April 2, 2000/Sunday, May 25, 1631 - The Ring of Fire takes place.

Fall 1632 - Gustav II Adolf and Mike Stearns organize the Confederated Principalities of Europe.

June 1634 - Congress of Copenhagen. Additional USE provinces are organized.

September 1634 - The Ram Rebellion concludes when the Ram takes von Bimbach's *schloss.*

September 1634 - Báner captures Ingolstadt via bribery.

January 1635 - Completion of the Capital Line railroad from Schwarza Junction to Magdeburg.

February 22, 1635 - United States of Europe and State of Thuringia-Franconia elections

- The Crown Loyalists win the election so Wilhelm Wettin will become the prime minister of the USE.

- Bamberg becomes the SoTF capital.

March 4, 1635 - The Dreeson Incident.

June 1635 - Wettin takes office; Gustav II Adolf appoints Mike Stearns a major general..

June 1635 - Krystalnacht - The Committees of Correspondence attack antisemites and witch hunters throughout the USE.

August 1635 - USE Army under Torstensson defeats the Saxons at Zwenkau; Swedish Army under Gustav II Adolf takes Brandenburg without a fight.

October 1635 - Swedish, Hessian, and USE forces invade the Polish-Lithuanian Commonwealth.

- After atrocities at the Battle of Swiebodzin, Stearns forms the Hangman Regiment under Jeff Higgins.

- Battles of Zielona Gora, Warta River, and Lake Bledno - Gustav II Adolf is injured.

October 1635 - Assassination of Queen Maria Eleanora.

January 1636 - Bavaria retakes Ingolstadt and invades the Oberpfalz.

February 1636 - Stearns and Third Division defeat Báner at the Battle of Ostra.

February 1636 - Gustav II Adolf recovers.

Terms, Concepts, and Groups of People

Committees of Correspondence (CoC) - organized to spread up-time ideals, leaders include Gretchen Richter, Gunter Achterhof, and Joachim von Thierbach ("Spartacus").

Confederated Principalities of Europe (CPE) - confederation of German states allied to Sweden, lasted from roughly October 1632 to October 1633.

Krystalnacht - The June 1635 NTL Committees of Correspondence campaign against antisemites and witch hunters. It's a deliberately ironic name meant to contrast with Kristallnacht, the 1938 OTL Nazi attack on Jews in Germany. While the series has not been completely consistent, we try to use a specific spelling for each.

New United States - Government of the Ring of Fire and adjoining areas. By August 1632, included all of southern Thuringia. Became part of the CPE in Fall 1633. Name changed to State of Thuringia in December 1633. Following elections in Franconia, name changed to State of Thuringia-Franconia (SoTF) in February 1634.

United States of Europe - successor to the CPE, although it is a nation rather than a confederation.

Contents

Introduction

The Magdeburg Messenger

(1632 Fiction)

This issue's cover story is "Cassini Rounds Third." Robert Waters continues the saga of Giovanni Cassini. Up-time, he was a famous astronomer. Down-time, he's a kid who wants to play ball. He might get to stay in Grantville, but is it really for the love of the game?

Next is Bethanne Kim's "A Fitting Tribute." The Ugolinis make memorial stones and other markers. That's not something the average down-timer is used to. Is there a way to save the family business?

Marc Tyrrell concludes "A Meeting at Midsummer" with Part 2. Paul, Gagnrad, Helmut, Captain von Thieren, and the Inquisitor Father Salazar are all on different missions. As most of their paths cross near Klettbach, which of them will succeed?

An evening at a very good restaurant leads to "A Disturbance at the Nishioka House." Garrett W. Vance's tale takes place immediately after "Ill-Met in the Marshes" from Issue 1. Plus, there's a cat.

The State Library Papers

(1632 Non-Fiction)

Iver P. Cooper's article "Something Old, Something New" is about construction materials and their availability (or lack thereof) in the new timeline.

Editor's Notes

Baen Books is starting to reissue 1632 books originally published by Ring of Fire Press. I have received editorial corrections for my first three books, and as I reviewed those, some thoughts came to mind.

First, the *Grantville Gazette* and Ring of Fire Press had style guides that were different from the 1632 series style guide that Baen Books maintains. A style guide provides precedent: "We did it this way in *1632*, so that's what we're going to keep doing." We published *Eric Flint's 1632 & Beyond* Issues 1 and 2 using largely the same style as *The Grantville Gazette*. After approving lots of editorial changes, one at a time, I want to regularize styles across the series.

So, beginning with this Issue 3 of *Eric Flint's 1632 & Beyond*:

AM and PM will become a.m. and p.m.

Spaced ellipses (. . .) will become the ellipsis character (...). In case you'd like to incorporate this yourself, it's alt0133.

We will continue to italicize foreign words...except when they are used in names or in direct address.

Names ending in -s will form the possessive with just the apostrophe: Joe's horse, but Lukas' horse.

The following words are not capitalized: basic training, tech center, tech school.

Gun belt and musket ball are each two words, but gunmaker and gunmaking are each one word.

The general format for bibliography entries is: Author. Title. Edition. City: Publisher, Year. Where cited in 1632 canon or on Baen's Bar. Comments.

In-line citations are simpler: either ("Short Work," Author, *Longer Work it's in*, Chapter or page number) or (*Title*, Author, Chapter or page number).

I am going to draw the line at the serial comma (Oxford comma). *Eric Flint's 1632 & Beyond* will use the serial comma for clarity, consistency, and to avoid confusion. (Do you see what I did there?)

Magdeburg Messenger
1632 Fiction

Flint's Shards, Inc.

Cassini Rounds Third

Robert E. Waters

Author's Note: This story is the fourth in the *Cassini Plays Ball* series. It follows the events in the previous three stories which were published in the Grantville Gazette: "Cassini at the Plate," (*Grantville Gazette* 93);"Cassini Takes First," (*Grantville Gazette* 96); and "Cassini Slides to Second" (*Grantville Gazette* 101).

"Never allow the fear of striking out keep you from playing the game."
–Babe Ruth

Game Two Against the Schwarzburg 4-Baggers
July 19, 1636

"Come on, boys." Coach Flannery clapped his hands while the team gathered their gear after the game. "Keep your spirits up. You lost, but you played hard, and that's what matters. I'm proud of you."

Giovanni Domenico Cassini was happy that Coach Flannery wasn't upset at their fourth loss of the season. A hard-fought loss, indeed–to the

Schwarzburg 4-Baggers, sadly. And after Giovanni had stolen his first base: man on second, in the scoring position, ready to earn that run. But no amount of speed or lead off the bag was going to keep a double play from happening two batters later. Giovanni didn't even reach third before the outs were called. Now, their record was two wins, four losses. A difficult hole from which to escape.

"We've got six games left. Six games. Keep playing hard, and we can pull this out."

Their next two were against the Rudolstadt Champions, the team that they had opened the season against, back in the early days when Giovanni was new to baseball and insecure. Now, he was a Grantville Mountaineer. There was no doubt about it, in his heart and his mind. Every loss was painful; every win, a joy. And not just for himself. He felt it for every player on the team, even annoying "Big Boy" Bobby Powers. He had never felt anything like this in his short life. He belonged here, in Grantville, and he could not imagine being anywhere else.

"Wanna come over?" Jerry Yost asked as their teammates drifted off to their other lives. "My mom's making pizza tonight."

"Pizza?" Giovanni was intrigued. He had never had pizza here in Grantville. He wondered if it was the same as the kind he had had in Perinaldo. Probably not. He nodded. "I'll ask Uncle Antonio. I'm sure he won't mind."

Uncle had been quite busy and—what did the up-timers call it?—preoccupied of late. His consultation work at the Koudsi Law Firm had been steady, but also, that woman—Lukas Shumpert's *mutter*—he'd seen them dining together. What was that all about? As much as he tried, he couldn't stop thinking about it.

Uncle Antonio came into view from up the street. Giovanni waved at him. "Just a minute, Jerry." He scampered off to ask if he could go home with his best friend.

He looked back at the field, at Jerry, at the few other remaining teammates waiting for their parents to arrive and pick them up. He smiled.

My team.

The Shumpert Household
July 20, 1636

Antonio Maria Crovese watched Luca Shumpert toil in her kitchen. Just tidying up, she had said, though the space was already immaculate. They hadn't been together long, but Antonio could tell, from the way she moved through the room, the way she mouthed silent words, that something weighed heavily on her mind.

"Come, my dear," Antonio said. "Let's go take a walk. It's a beautiful day. Let me take your mind off these domestic duties."

"Walk?" Luca said as she rubbed down the same countertop for the third time. "And be seen in public?"

"Ah." Antonio stepped carefully across the room. He slid his arm around her waist, buried his face in her neck, and kissed the soft skin below the hairline. "That's what's troubling you." He kissed her again. "We've already been seen, my love. We have dined together."

"That was different." Luca turned in his arms, leaned against the sink. She patted Antonio's shoulders, flashed a smile. "That was for work."

Officially, she was correct, but as far as Antonio was concerned, those meals were far, far more than just two co-workers talking law.

Luca pulled away from him. "It's just that...I think it best that I tell Lukas first. Learning that his father is not coming back, and that I am with someone new. I—I think he should know first before we take things any further. He deserves to know."

Antonio nodded. It was the right thing to do, he supposed. He needed to tell Giovanni as well. His nephew was a very bright boy. He probably had already figured out that something was going on with the woman he had seen his uncle dining with the other night.

"Very well." He leaned against the sink. "I guess the question after that, then, is what comes next?" He smiled and winked. "You and Lukas could return to Perinaldo with me and Giovanni."

Luca huffed. She picked up a dish towel and reached for a cup soaking in soapy water. "Impossible. Our lives are here, Antonio. My work. All of Lukas' friends." She sighed, dried the cup, and set it aside. She teared up. "Maybe I should say nothing. It'll all be over once their season is finished. You and Giovanni will be heading back to Italy after that, won't you?"

Antonio felt a sinking feeling in his chest. It was a sensation he wasn't used to, nor liked. When he looked at Luca, he could think of nothing else, and all his troubles, his uncertainties of the future, bled away. Yes, once the Mountaineers' season was over—and that would be very soon—the natural course of action would be to return to Italy. They had only come here for a short stay anyway, right? There was never a thought of staying for very long. But...

He took Luca in his arms. She stopped her cleaning, turned, and sank into his chest. Antonio closed his eyes. She felt so good against him. So good.

"Well," he said, "what if Giovanni and I stay here, in Grantville, with you and Lukas, forever?"

Higgins Hotel Dining Room
July 21

Antonio could tell that his nephew was troubled; he sighed quietly. The second person in as many days whose emotional discomfort he'd have to divine.

"So," he said, "your next two games are in Rudolstadt, yes?"

Giovanni nodded. "Yes."

Antonio raised his head and looked up at the dining room ceiling. He squinted. "As I recall, you won your first game against them."

"Yes. Lost the second, though."

"Are you confident in your chances against them now?"

Giovanni shrugged and flipped his fork through his mashed potatoes. "I guess."

Antonio grunted and scooped up his final morsel of potatoes. "Rudolstadt isn't very far by train. You're leaving tomorrow, ten in the morning, yes?"

Giovanni nodded.

This time, Antonio sighed loudly and set his fork down, perhaps a little more forcefully than he wanted. "All right, what is the matter, young man? You have been moping around all evening. What's wrong?"

It took a good full minute before Giovanni answered. "Coach Flannery is thinking about putting Bobby Powers back on first, now that his leg has healed enough."

"All right."

Giovanni looked at his uncle, an annoyed expression on his face. He pointed a finger at his chest. "I'm playing first!"

1632 & BEYOND ISSUE 3

Oh, right. How foolish, but Antonio had momentarily forgotten, what with everything going on in his own life these days. *Focus, Antonio. Focus...* "What does that mean?"

"It means that I'll be sitting on the bench again. I'll be lucky even to bat."

That wasn't good. They hadn't come all the way to Grantville just to—well, they hadn't come to Grantville to play baseball at all, in fact. They had come to give Giovanni an opportunity to see how his life, his professional career as an astronomer, engineer, mathematician, would evolve, how he would become one of the premier scientists in the world as per the evidence on full display in the Grantville library. But life had carried them in another direction, as it often did. Life had certainly changed for Antonio, even more so than for Giovanni, in many ways. In the end, his bright nephew could still be a famous astronomer despite his current love for baseball. For Antonio, however, time was running out. He wasn't an old man, in the strict sense, but he wasn't a boy either. He didn't have much more time to find—*God forgive my silliness*—the love of his life. Had he found it in Luca? Antonio wasn't sure, but one thing was certain: he couldn't find that out if he returned to Italy without her.

He finished the last of his dinner and pushed his plate away. "I'm sure Coach Flannery will do right by you, Giovanni. You have earned your place on the team." He cleared his throat, wiped his mouth clean, and continued. "But perhaps I have news that will brighten your spirits.

"What do you think about staying here, in Grantville, on a more permanent basis?"

That, indeed, perked the boy's spirits. His head shot up, his eyes widened, a smile crossed his lips. "Really?"

Antonio nodded. "Yes. My work with the Koudsi Law Firm is going well. I don't know if I can maintain a permanent position with them, but if not, I'm certain there are other law firms—even businesses—here in Grantville or nearby that would be interested in legal consultation. My knowledge of Italian mercantile law is worth—"

"Wait," Giovanni blurted. He scrunched his brow in a clear indication that he was working something out in his mind. Finally, he said, "Is this about the lady I saw you with the other night?"

Antonio snickered. Smart boy. "Some of it, yes. I have...begun a relationship with her. I'm very fond of her."

"But, isn't she Lukas' mother?"

Antonio's heart sank. He didn't want to answer, but with the proverbial cat having scurried out of the bag, he saw no reason to lie. Besides, Giovanni would see right through any hesitation or obfuscation on his part. "Yes. How do you know that?"

"I saw her the other day at the game. I thought it was the same woman that I saw you with, but—"

"Yes," Antonio said, hoping to end this part of the conversation quickly. "She is Lukas' mother. She works at the law firm with me. She's a very nice lady, Giovanni, and I would like to stay in Grantville with her."

"But Lukas speaks of his father all the time. He tells us that his father is a soldier in the 3rd Division of the USE army, that he serves Michael Stearns. That he's fighting against the Ottomans, and that he will be home someday and—"

"Life, young man," Antonio said, interrupting, begging God that this conversation would conclude, "is not always that simple. As I understand it, his father is gone, and he will not be returning. But that is not your concern. You let me worry about my relationship with Luca; you focus on your future. Do you wish to remain in Grantville after the season, or do you wish to return to Perinaldo?"

It wasn't fair to place such a momentous decision on the boy, Antonio knew. Giovanni was, in fact, too young to make such a choice on his own.

He was a child, and as such, the decision rested upon those sworn to raise and protect him. What was best for the boy was the question Antonio should be asking himself.

There was no easy answer for that, either.

"Yes, I want to stay." His brow curled up again. "But what about *mia madre, mio padre*?"

Antonio nodded. "I will send them word of our decision to remain. It will take time for them to get the word, but I'm sure that, when I explain to them the wonderful educational opportunities for you here, they will agree." He shrugged. "Perhaps they may even come to pay a visit."

The Shumpert Household
July 21, 1636

Luca Shumpert could barely contain her tears as she told her son about his father. "He—he isn't coming back, Lukas. We have heard no word from him for almost six months. Before that, we were always getting word. It has stopped, and there can be no other explanation: he isn't coming back."

She waited to see if Lukas would say something, ask a question. He wanted to; she could tell from his confused expression, but like her, he was trying to be brave, trying not to cry in front of his mother.

Finally, he said, "No, I don't believe you. He would not do that to us."

"Lukas." Luca tried to keep her anxiety, her frustration, in check. She closed her eyes, took a breath, then opened them. "We must face the truth. It has been six months. Other wives, other mothers, have had word from their husbands, their sons, from the front. The same front your father fights upon. He has not sent us word in over six months.

"I have prayed to God every day for word, but my prayers have not been answered. The reason is clear to me now: he is not coming back. And we must accept that, as painful as it is. We must."

"Is he dead?"

The question struck her heart like a knife. She shook her head. "I do not know, my sweet boy. I cannot decide, in truth, what answer to that question is the best. Is he alive? Dead? I pray for the former, but I just do not know."

She reached for him, to pull him close into an embrace, as much for herself as for Lukas. He let her, though she could tell by his stiffness that he was angry, confused, not ready yet to accept the truth of her words.

She hugged him tightly, dreading the next thing she had to tell him. But the truth was the best. Get it all out now, before he learns of it from someone that is *not* his mother.

She pulled away but kept hold of his arms. She looked Lukas square in the face, trying to show strength. "There is something else I must tell you.

"I've—I've been seeing another man, someone that perhaps you know. His name is Antonio Maria Crovese." She swallowed, careful to measure her next words. "He is Giovanni Cassini's uncle."

Lukas pulled away. "Giovanni? What do you mean?"

"I have been spending time with Antonio. He is a very nice man. He has been working with Laura at the law firm. He has been giving her counsel on Italian mercantile law. I met him the first day he came to the office. He is a very nice man. I think you would like him. I—"

"No!" Lukas shouted, tearing himself away from his mother's grasp. "This is shit!"

"Lukas! Watch your language!"

"No!" he shouted again, stepping away from her. Now his tears began to flow. "Giovanni is just a stupid little boy from Italy. And my father is not dead. He did not leave us. He will come back."

He turned from her and fled into his room. Before he slammed the door shut, he shouted, "hure" at the top of his voice.

Whore. Luca could not believe that her own son had just called her a whore.

Perhaps I am, she thought, falling onto her couch, pulling up her legs and hugging them tight, not holding back her tears either.

Perhaps I am.

Game Three Against the Rudolstadt Champions
July 22, 1636

Rudolstadt was the first train stop north of the Schwarza Junction on the so-called Capital Line from Grantville to Magdeburg. A short trip but one that felt like a million miles to Cassini. A million miles with no reward at the end.

Coach Flannery tried sounding positive. "Your batting has improved greatly, Mr. Cassini. Let Bobby worry about first base while you concentrate on hitting. I'll make sure you get your fair share of bats before you go back to Italy. I promise."

Of course, he wasn't going back to Italy, but nobody knew that yet. He hadn't told anyone, not even Jerry. He was dying to tell his best friend, but the moment didn't seem right. This matter with Bobby, and who would command first base, had to be resolved before he could even think about spreading the good news. Now that the matter was resolved, it still didn't feel right.

Jerry patted him on the back. "Don't worry about it, Gio." Jerry had gotten into the habit of shortening Giovanni's name. "You did great on first. I'm sure Coach will let you pinch hit once in a while."

Once in a while was not what Giovanni wanted, but now that the decision was as good as made, what could he do about it? His preference would be to pinch run, maybe even for Big Boy himself. That made the most sense. As he and his teammates stepped off the train and into wagons ready to take them the short distance to the local Little League diamond, Giovanni made a mental note to ask the coach just that.

The Rudolstadt Champions' field was nothing but a cow pasture smoothed and leveled for baseball. As they climbed out of the wagons and into the visiting team's makeshift dugout (which was just a row of crates assembled for sitting purposes), Mountaineer catcher Alex Dorrman made a snide remark to Bobby Powers. "Hey, Big Boy...watch out for them cows!"

Everyone laughed, including Giovanni. In his unique style, Bobby gave Alex the bird. "Bite me!" Giovanni marveled at the size of the digit. Even Bobby's fingers were huge.

The Mountaineers batted first, but the inning ended in one ground out, one strikeout, and a pop fly. The Champions fared no better. Mountaineer Aaron Rollison Wendell was pitching nothing but strikes, proving that he was one of the best pitchers in the league. Despite their name, the Champions had little in the way of strong batters, and rumor had it that they had lost three of their starters recently, down-time boys who had just walked off the team. All that the Mountaineers needed for a win were some hits and runs.

Bobby came up to bat at the top of the fourth, with the score one to zip, Mountaineers. Jerry got on base and then scored at the top of the second on a ground out error as the ball popped up at just the right moment and smacked the third baseman in the shin. Jerry made it home with ease. Now Bobby stood there, cocky as ever, pointing his bat to center field, daring the Rudolstadt pitcher to do his worst.

Giovanni sat beside Lukas. The Mountaineer third baseman had been quiet and pensive the entire trip from Grantville. "Are you up next?" He asked.

Lukas shook his head. "No. Elias is up next."

"If we get a couple more runs, I think we'll win."

Lukas grunted.

Bobby let the first pitch go by. "Ball!" the umpire said, making the proper motion. Bobby adjusted for the second pitch and waited.

"He's a pain, but I hope Bobby will—"

"Leave me alone!"

Lukas stood and went down the line of crates to sit next to Alex. Giovanni sat there, mouth open, not certain that he had heard Lukas right. *Why is he mad? I didn't say anything wrong.*

Bobby swung and struck the second pitch, a high-flying arch into center field. Bobby's running had improved as his leg had improved, but he was still one of the slowest boys on the Mountaineers.

He took off to first base. All eyes were on the pop fly and the small Rudolstadt boy trying to find it in the sunlight. The ball began to descend. Down, down, down it fell. The Rudolstadt outfielder tried adjusting as the ball came dangerously close to reaching and then breaching the demarcation line that had been set up to denote home runs. Giovanni was on his feet, cheering Bobby forward, knowing—perhaps more so than anyone else at the game—that the ball was not going to reach the line. It was going to fall short.

And so it did. Its drop ended about five feet from the line as the Rudolstadt outfielder put up his glove, shielded his eyes from the sun as best as he could, and made a grab for the ball. For a second, it seemed as if he'd caught it, and all of Bobby's huffing and puffing would be for nothing. But then the ball dropped from the boy's glove and onto the ground.

The Mountaineers cheered as Bobby took first base. He did not try for a double.

"Time!" Coach Flannery said, waving at the umpire.

Time was called, and Coach Flannery waved Giovanni in.

"Mr. Cassini, you'll pinch run for Mr. Powers."

Giovanni smiled and saluted in the style he had seen some up-timers do. "Good decision, Mr. Flannery, Coach, sir."

Flannery smiled, removed his cap, and gave Giovanni a gentle tap with it on the shoulder. "Try to steal second if you can."

Giovanni was all for that.

He took first, turned, and saw Lukas scowling at him from the dugout. And suddenly, Giovanni understood why Lukas was in such a foul mood. *He knows.*

Grantville Mountaineers' Campground, Rudolstadt

Brooks Robinson. Brooks Robinson. Brooks Robinson. The name echoed through Giovanni's mind. He stared at Lukas across the bonfire as the rest of the team celebrated their three-to-zero victory over the Champions. Their easiest win to date.

Coach Flannery had invited the opposing team to a cookout—to help spread good will and teamwork throughout the league, he said. The Champions' coaches had agreed, and here they were, both teams mingling about the fire, roasting "hot dogs" over the flames, talking, telling corny jokes, laughing, playing catch, you name it. But not Giovanni, and not Lukas either, who had spent the last several minutes digging through the burning ash of the fire with a scorched stick, doing his best to ignore the noise and activity all around them. Giovanni tried to do the same, though Jerry's calls to "come play catch with us" were quite tempting. But not yet. Not until he had figured out a way to talk to Lukas.

Giovanni got up and walked slowly, casually around the bonfire, acting as if he were just strolling through a park. When he got close to Lukas, he said carefully, "You played well today, Lukas. Just like Brooks Robinson."

Lukas said nothing at first, kept making Xs and Os in the smoldering ash with his stick. Finally, he acknowledged the comment. "What do you know about Robinson?"

Giovanni risked taking a seat on the small pile of wood at Lukas' left. "Not a lot, but I've heard you talk about him to Jerry and Aaron.

"Brooks Robinson is your most favorite up-time ball player," Giovanni continued. "You have at least two baseball cards of the man. He played for the Baltimore Orioles for 23 seasons, and he was called 'The Human Vacuum Cleaner' by many, even you, because he was considered the greatest defensive third baseman in the history of the game."

Giovanni smiled. "I guess we should start calling you The Vacuum Cleaner now, eh? Stretching out like you did in the last inning, to catch that low zinger. That was a great move."

Lukas grunted, shrugged, kept digging in the ash. "Thanks. It's easy to play good against a team like the Champions. I didn't do much."

They sat there, in silence, for a long while. Jerry called to Giovanni again. "Well, I guess I'll go and meet some of the Rudolstadt players. You want to come?"

Lukas shook his head. "No, I'm okay here."

As Giovanni stood and turned away, Lukas muttered, "My dad is dead."

That stopped him. He turned back, paused, not knowing what to say.

"He's dead," Lukas said more forcefully, dropping the stick. "My mother said so. We haven't heard from him in a long time. He's not coming back."

Lukas sprang up and ran into the darkness. Giovanni wanted to follow, to find him, to try to comfort him in any way he could. But how could he? What could he do? What could he say? Giovanni's father was alive. His mother. His uncle. He didn't know how to feel about Lukas' distress. They weren't best friends. They weren't really friends at all, not like he and Jerry were.

"I'm sorry," Giovanni said weakly through the growing darkness. "I'm sorry."

Game Four Against the Rudolstadt Champions
July 22, 1636

Game four against the Champions proved more difficult, as the previous evening's festivities had worn heavily on the Mountaineers' concentration.

"Why ain't the Champions tired?" Bobby Powers wondered as he huffed it back to the "dugout" after having his massive pop fly snatched out of the sky with ease. He tossed his bat aside.

"They must have slipped us mickeys," James Matthew Shaver said, getting ready to take center field. His performance was seriously lacking today.

"In what? Our hot dogs?"

It was a funny question, but no one laughed. Everyone was too tired to even crack a smile.

Luckily, they were down by only one run. Giovanni felt compelled to try to raise their spirits.

"Come on, guys." He tried to emulate their coach. "Let's not lose heart. We're down by only one run. We can win this."

"Who are you now?" Bobby asked. "Our coach?"

Coach Flannery was over by the umpire, arguing a call. It did little good, and Giovanni could see that the ump was about to blow his stack. Coach Flannery finally backed off and stormed away, mumbling some kind of curse word under his breath. He reached the dugout and began clapping loudly.

"Okay, okay!" He accentuated each word of affirmation with a loud, sharp clap. "Bottom of the sixth, and one run behind. Let's get out there and hustle. Put this inning behind us. Don't give them another run." He pointed at Aaron. "Mr. Wendell, when their best hitter, Tobias, gets on the plate, I want him walked." He pointed at Alex. "Alex, I want you to—"

Coach Flannery went down the line, giving each player instructions. As he did so, Giovanni dared slide up to Lukas. He said nothing. He just sat there. The coach gave Lukas his instructions. The umpire called for the Mountaineers to take to the field. "Okay, now," Coach Flannery said. "Get out there and finish this inning!"

"Good luck," Giovanni said, giving Lukas a gentle pat on the shoulder.

Lukas paused, turned, and said, "Yeah, you too."

* * *

The bottom of the sixth was a challenge to put away, but they did so on a lucky bounce into second baseman Elias Becker's glove. As Coach Flannery directed, they walked Tobias, struck out the next batter, then all hell broke loose, as Bobby might say. A squeaker between second and third, missed by Jerry who lunged for it, but failed to connect, put Tobias on second. Like Bobby Powers, Tobias was big, lanky, and relatively slow. Nevertheless, with only one out and a man on first and second, the chances for the Champions to score on another single went up by...what? Twenty percent? Thirty? Fifty? Maybe much higher. Giovanni tried calculating the numbers in his mind as he prepared to bat at the top of the seventh and final inning. His research about the physics of baseball at the Grantville library had not given him those statistics. Nevertheless, with only one man out and first and second occupied, the chance for the Champions to score and, in effect, put the game out of Mountaineer reach, was high.

That lucky bounce came with the next batter, a tall, thin fellow who served the Champions in center field. His swing was strong, but his timing was off. He struck the third pitch hard, but instead of the ball flying over Elias' reach, it tracked low, bounced twice, and then struck second base itself. Tobias, assuming he had an easy path to third, was caught off guard and off base. The ball struck the bag and popped right into Elias' glove. He tagged Tobias out quickly, and then threw to first. Double play.

Now, it was the top of the seventh, and Giovanni was up first, pinch hitting for their top pitcher, Aaron Rollison Wendell. Lukas was up second.

"I'll get to second, Lukas," Giovanni said, as he prepared to bat, "and you hit me home."

Lukas grunted. "Don't count on it. I've not been very good today."

That was true. A ground out and a pop fly. But nobody was playing well today. "You'll do it. I know you can."

Lukas nodded and tried to flash a smile. "I'll try, Gio. Good luck to you."

Giovanni had watched the Champions' pitcher all day. He was good. A small boy, but seemingly strong. Good control. His signature pitch was a fastball straight down the middle, but on occasion, he tried a slider, a curve. Sometimes, it worked. Sometimes, it curled wildly off the mark. The Champions' coach had decided, much to Giovanni's surprise, not to change pitchers, even though the young man's strength and control were beginning to wane. Was it because they had no other pitcher right now on their roster? Giovanni didn't know, but he hoped to take advantage of that here in the final inning.

First pitch was a high fastball. Giovanni let it pass by.

"Ball!"

The second was another fastball, low and inside. Giovanni swung at it and clipped it to the right.

"Strike!"

In his peripheral, he could see the Champions' catcher's fingers moving madly below his catcher's mitt. It was either a ruse or a sincere request for the pitcher to give Giovanni something new, a slider or a curve. He had watched the catcher make these signals throughout the game, and the pitcher had always responded with a different pitch. He doubted that now, suddenly, the Champions would be pulling a ruse to fool him. He doubted that they possessed that kind of imagination.

He waited, crouching, his bat up, his eyes firmly on the pitcher's throwing hand. The wind up, the wind up, and then the throw.

Yep, it was a slider, and from what Giovanni had observed throughout the game, it always broke to the left. He waited, watched the pitch break, raised his bat a fraction more, then swung.

He struck the ball clean. A metal pop off the aluminum bat, and the ball floated over the line between first and second. The second baseman tried reaching for it, but it soared just over his glove, landed on the ground, and bounced into shallow right field.

The Mountaineer fans in attendance cheered as Giovanni reached first base easily. He made a few moves towards second, but then backpedaled immediately as the ball did not bounce far enough to secure a double.

"That's how it's done, Gio!" Jerry shouted from the dugout. "Come on, Lukas. Send him home!"

Lukas Shumpert stepped to the plate. Giovanni gave him a look, nodded, clapped, and repeated what Jerry had said. Lukas nodded, made his adjustments, and stepped into the batter's box.

His face was blank, almost serene, granite-like. No expression, save for a twitch of his lip as if he were about to burst into tears. His look chilled Giovanni. It was an expression of anger. A controlled anger, as if Lukas were pushing all his pain, his frustration, into his bat. And the bat would be a conduit through which all his emotions would flow. Giovanni could almost feel Lukas' hands on his throat as the Mountaineer third baseman gripped his bat and waited for the pitch.

First pitch, low and inside. Lukas swung and fouled it to the right. Second pitch, much the same. Third time, however, the angry boy put all his strength into it, struck it true, and sent it up and into left field.

Giovanni gasped as he ran towards second, his eyes on the ball as it soared through the air and toward the home run line. Even Bobby Powers couldn't have hit the ball any harder. Lukas had put a serious hurt on this one, and it was going yard.

Giovanni made second base and kept going as the ball soared over the home run line.

The Mountaineer fans, and the Mountaineers in the dugout, went wild.

* * *

A double by the Champions in the bottom of the seventh gave the Mountaineers pause. However, their defense held, and the side (and the game) was closed. The Mountaineers won two to one. A squeaker, but the win had pulled their record up to even for the season: four wins, four losses.

There was much celebration on the train back to Grantville. Coach Flannery was beside himself with joy, glad-handing everyone, patting backs, cracking jokes, and whistling in a high-pitched squeal that hurt Giovanni's ears. But he didn't care. What mattered to him the most, even more so than the wins, was Lukas' change of demeanor. He was, as up-timers might say, a rock star.

Everyone wanted to shake his hand, pat him on the back. Even Bobby, who rarely admitted that anyone else on the team could hit a home run like him, couldn't deny Lukas' power in that one swing. "As you've told us a million times," Bobby said to Lukas, rolling his eyes, slapping him a little too hard on the shoulder, "Brooks Robinson hit 268 home runs in his career. Now, you have your first. Don't screw it up!"

Giovanni had managed to weasel his way next to Lukas as the train trundled forward, the German landscape blurry outside their window. The train was moving faster than any man could run, for certain. They'd be back in Grantville very soon.

It was Lukas who spoke first, changing the subject, much to Giovanni's surprise. "So," he said, "maybe you and I and your uncle and my mom can do something someday. Like, have a picnic or something."

Giovanni nodded. "Sure. Our next two games are in Grantville. We should have time. I'll ask Uncle Antonio when we get back."

That seemed to settle the situation for now, though Giovanni could see, underneath Lukas's smiling face and sudden jovial attitude, that the reality of his father's death still weighed heavily upon his mind. It seemed as if he were trying to reconcile with the reality of it but was having trouble doing so.

Giovanni turned back to the window and watched the world fly by.

The Shumpert Household
July 24, 1636

Antonio was happy. Perhaps happier than he had ever been. The sun shone brightly, a comforting breeze blew through the Shumperts' backyard, meat cooked on a charcoal grill (which Luca had borrowed from an up-time neighbor), and the boys were playing cornhole. That, perhaps more than anything else, mattered the most.

"Lukas seems to have taken the news well." Antonio stood near the grill with spatula in hand, waiting a few minutes more before flipping the meat. "I admire his courage."

"He's hurt," Luca said, leaning into Antonio and laying her head upon his shoulder. "He's angry with me. I was too frank with him, too abrupt. I should have taken more time, been more...delicate in my words." She huffed. "Here I am, working in a law firm, and I could not find the right words to tell him about his father."

"He will be all right. He is a strong young man. He will be fine, in time."

Antonio flipped the meat, four searing chunks of beef that he had purchased from a local grocery store. Cut potatoes and carrots boiled in a pot nearby. They, too, were nearly ready for some butter and seasoning. It was going to be a splendid meal, finished off with a quart of so-called "Italian Ice" which he had also picked up from a local ice cream parlor. And then, finally, an up-time movie that Luca said, "You have got to see." Very well, then, he'd try it. Anything for her.

With a cooking mitt on her right hand, Luca grabbed the handle of the pot containing the potatoes and carrots and sloshed it around. She then picked up a long fork and poked it into the boiling water, stabbing a soft chunk of potato. She nodded. "Almost ready." She set the fork aside, took off her protective glove. "So, have you considered my offer?"

Antonio smiled, leaned his face towards hers, and gave her a quick peck on the cheek. "Are you sure you want us to? Moving in together is a big step forward. And we are not married yet, my love. Wouldn't it be prudent if we first—"

"This is Grantville, a modern town. No one will concern themselves with our living arrangements."

Perhaps that was so, and perhaps not. He was certainly ready to move in with her, to pack up his and Giovanni's belongings at the hotel and start this new life with Luca and Lukas. He could do it right after dinner. He'd be there and back in less than an hour. He wanted to do so very badly, but... "I have not discussed this with Giovanni yet. I think it would be best if I did so first."

Luca shrugged. "Then, let's discuss it during dinner."

* * *

Cornhole was a fun game, Giovanni admitted, but like all physical games, it boiled down to physics: when to toss the bag, where to toss it, and how hard to toss it. Giovanni had an eye for it, but for these games, he had allowed Lukas to win two of three. So far, at least. Three out of five was the goal. Game four was very close.

Lukas stepped up to the toss line, drew his arm back, paused, then let the tiny red bean bag fly towards its mark. A little too fast, Giovanni noticed, as the bag twirled and twirled. It hit the angled board, and slid up towards the hole, but didn't quite make it.

"One point," Giovanni said, hefting his own white bags. One of them had apparently broken open and had been resewn, making it a kind of impediment to the quality of his throws. He had to compensate for this "gimp" bag, as Lukas called it, by tossing it a little higher and a little harder. No worries. Easy-peasy.

Giovanni stepped up to the toss line. He gripped the gimpy bag. Problem was, Lukas' last throw had put his bag in a blocking position. If Giovanni wasn't careful with this throw, it would likely knock Lukas' into the hole, scoring him three points and possibly giving him the win. Lukas winning the match would be fine. *But,* Giovanni grinned to himself, *let him earn it at least.*

The trick, then, was to toss it in such a way that it sailed over Lukas' bag and either scored a hole in one, or struck the board above the hole, and then slid in. Doing that would be a challenge, even for Giovanni. Perhaps it would be best to simply strike the board and score one point, end the game in a tie, and force a tiebreaker.

No. There was no reason to do that. What did up-timer baseball giant Babe Ruth say about the fear of striking out? This toss would either win the game outright for Giovanni or win it for Lukas. Either way, he'd be satisfied, and no fear either way would be felt.

He breathed deeply, pulled his arm back, waited for the breeze to settle, then let fly.

Like a baseball, the bean bag was white, and like a pop fly, it arched into the sky, a little higher than Giovanni had hoped for, but the toss was straight and true. It began to descend. Both boys leaned forward, their eyes fixed on the bag, as it finally, after many agonizing seconds, hit the board. Right near where Giovanni had hoped it would strike.

But not as true as he had hoped. The bag struck the board, and then slid away from the hole. It teetered there on the lip of the board—teetered, teetered—and then fell to the ground.

"I win!" Lukas shouted, clapping his hands once and then smiling ear to ear. "Let's play again."

Giovanni was about to agree when his uncle called, "Giovanni, Lukas...come and eat!"

They all gathered at the table that Luca had prepared in the backyard. Antonio served the meal, Luca served cool drinks, and they began to eat.

They talked about the upcoming games with the Saalfeld Dukes. Lukas seemed unconcerned with the match-up; Giovanni was the opposite. According to Coach Flannery, the Dukes were every bit as good as the Schwarzburg 4-Baggers, and in fact, perhaps even better these days. They and the 4-Baggers were fighting for the top spot. It would be a challenging two- game series, but everyone at the table was glad that they were home games. Uncle Antonio made a promise then and there to attend both of them, especially now that his contract with the Koudsi Law Firm was coming to a close. That, too, became a topic of conversation, as Lukas' mother and Uncle Antonio discussed where he might find another job.

On the way back from Rudolstadt, Giovanni had finally told everyone that he was staying in Grantville permanently. Jerry had been quite pleased with the announcement, and most others on the team were as well, including Coach Flannery. Bobby Powers said very little, though Giovanni hoped that that tiny little grin he had noticed on Big Boy's face was due to the announcement. Maybe so, maybe not. Nevertheless, the truth was out there now, and so Uncle Antonio needed to keep working. But where? Perhaps he could stay at Koudsi, although that didn't seem likely. Other law firms were discussed. Giovanni found the conversation quite interesting; Lukas, less so.

Finally, they talked about enrolling Giovanni into school. Uncle Antonio would have to get that process started soon. Baseball season was coming to a close. Classes would begin within a month or so, and Giovanni couldn't wait. He was growing just as excited about that as he had been about playing baseball, for starting classes meant that it was real, that they would stay in Grantville, that Perinaldo was—as an up-timer might say—in the rearview mirror. He would miss his mother and father, yes, but he couldn't wait to start school. Despite his love for baseball, Giovanni's "intellectual curiosity," as Uncle Antonio called it, was something he had to feed.

Dinner concluded. Giovanni was stuffed. He couldn't possibly eat another bite, although when Luca brought out the Italian ice, he suddenly found room in his much-crowded stomach.

Luca scooped the ice into four bowls, took a seat, and shot a glance toward Uncle Antonio. "Antonio, do you have something you'd like to say to these young men?"

Antonio gobbled down a spoonful of cold, delicious goodness. He nodded, swallowed, put down his spoon, and sighed. He folded his hands together and said, "Giovanni, Lukas, there is something that we would like to discuss with you."

Game Three Against the Saalfeld Dukes
July 25, 1636

"Hey, Cassini!" Bobby shouted as the team prepared to take the field against the Saalfeld Dukes. "I hear your uncle has the hots for Shumpert's mama. Ooh la la!"

Giovanni had never heard Bobby giggle, but there he went, snickering like a villain rubbing his hands together with devious satisfaction.

"Oh, pipe down, Big Boy," Jerry barked, putting on his glove and stepping onto the field. "Ain't none of your business."

There was a pause. Giovanni considered responding to Bobby's teasing, but the big guy continued. "Well, at least you're staying here in Grantville and not going back to the boot. Pay me money, and I'll be your bodyguard in school."

Bobby shed another barrage of giggles, got his arm punched by Jerry, a stern "Enough chit-chat! Take the field!" from Coach Flannery, and finally he shut up. The Mountaineers took their positions, and the game began.

Lukas hadn't shown up, however. Coach Flannery waited as long as he could to see if he'd show up, but he didn't. The game was beginning, and the coach had to make a decision.

"You'll sub for Mr. Shumpert, Gio," he said, now using the shortened version as well. "At least until he arrives...if he arrives. You've got base experience. Third base is different from first, but you'll do fine."

Where was Lukas? The cookout went well. Cornhole was fun. Lukas even seemed to be all right with the idea that Giovanni and Uncle Antonio would, soon, move into their home. It had been a great night. So, where was he?

But, of course, Uncle Antonio was on his way, as promised. First, however, he would drop by Lukas' home and pick up Luca, and they would come to the game together. So, maybe Lukas was just waiting to arrive then. Uncle Antonio was running a little late, but he'd be here. There was no reason for him to miss it.

Giovanni took third. It was a strange feeling being all the way across the field from first base. This whole side of the field felt different, vacuous. Coach Flannery was right: it was different. Jerry told him that playing third was almost like being a shortstop, and that a lot of balls were hit between third and second base. "You'll have to get used to stretching," Jerry said.

But that wouldn't be necessary. Lukas would be here soon.

* * *

Antonio greeted everyone he met along his walk with a nod and tip of his felt hat. He was dressed well today, having just completed his work at the Koudsi Law Firm. Now, he was headed to Luca's home. The day was slightly overcast, but no rain threatened. So, why not wear one's best? He hadn't attended one of Giovanni's games in a while, so it was right and proper to arrive in good clothing, good form, and ready to enjoy the day. The only troubling thing was that Luca hadn't come into the office this morning.

"A little under the weather," she had said on her call into the office. Hopefully, not so under the weather that she couldn't come with him to the game. Today's game would be their first official outing as a legitimate Grantville couple. Not only was he excited about finally revealing his relationship to God and the world, but the boys would be excited about it too. Especially Giovanni, who was overjoyed to be staying in Grantville after the season. Today was the start of their new life.

The Shumpert house was quiet and still when he arrived. The drapes were pulled shut, he noticed. Lukas had probably left for the game a while ago. Antonio stepped up to the front door, but paused before knocking. If Luca was too sick to attend the game, then he'd go on his own. He'd prefer to stay with her and comfort her in her illness, but he had made a promise to his nephew. He wasn't going to miss this one.

He knocked on the door, stepped back, adjusted his vest and hat, and placed a big smile on his face. Immediately, he regretted not bringing flowers, but he'd make it up to her after the game.

No one answered the door. He knocked again. He knocked a third time. He leaned forward and opened his mouth, ready to say her name through the door.

The door opened. It was a man similar in height to Antonio but standing higher due to the stoop. Over his right eye was a white cloth with faint streaks of dried blood. His face was covered in black-gray stubble. His clothing was common, unassuming. He held his left foot up, suggesting a sprained ankle, and he leaned on a crutch tucked beneath his left arm. "Yes, can I help you?"

His voice was gruff and heavily accented. Antonio paused, closed his mouth, reflexively removed his hat, and stood straight. He cleared his throat. "Yes, I'm...I'm here to see Luca Shumpert."

The man stared at him, winced in pain as he adjusted his stance. "To whom am I speaking, sir?"

"I am Antonio Maria Crovese," he said. "I...I work with Luca at the Koudsi Law Firm." He swallowed. "To whom am I speaking, sir?"

The man stood as straight as he could. "Gerhart Shumpert, Luca's husband."

A Fitting Tribute

Bethanne Kim

M y dad introduced me to the 1632 series, and we enjoyed it together for many years. This particular story is for my beloved father, may he rest in peace.

Grantville

October 1635

Angela Ugolini wrapped her coat tighter and leaned against her husband, Alberto, glad to be wearing wool stockings and several layers of skirts along with an irreplaceable pair of up-time muck boots she guarded zealously lest they be damaged. "Honey, he lived a good life."

"That is such a cliché. I mean, he did live a good life, but when your family business is making memorials, there are some things you hear all the time from grieving family. 'He lived a good life.' 'She was a good woman.' 'He, or she, died too young.' 'They lived a full life.' It doesn't make them untrue, but he was my Dad. You know?"

"I know, honey, you want it to be different, but you've been in this business long enough to know that at some level, it's all the same."

Alberto nodded, tears sliding down his cheeks as he looked, unseeing, at his parents' tombstone.

Domenica Allegrezza Ugolini

Devoted Wife and Mother

1940–1996

The other side was blank, the stone awaiting the words he never expected to be carving quite so soon:

Alberto Ugolini, Sr.

Devoted Husband and Father

1939 – 1635

Before they walked home, Alberto put his hand on the headstone and spoke, his voice a whispered vow. "Papa, I promise I will find a way to keep your business going."

December 1635

Her last pair of up-time earplugs in place, Angela steeled herself and opened the books. *At least I'm not looking at pages of red ink. Of course, that's only because we can't afford to buy red ink.* The expenses of Alberto Sr.'s final illness hadn't been excessive as those things go, but the business hadn't been doing well for years. Europe was old, and so were its cemeteries. All but the richest people eventually had their bones removed from their grave and reinterred elsewhere to allow the recently deceased to be buried. This led to a distinct lack of business for a company selling headstones, footstones, and other permanent (stone) memorials. But it was December, and she and Alberto were determined that Christmas bonuses would be paid. If they had to, they had even agreed they would ask Gabi for enough to cover them. Better for their pride to suffer a bit than for their employees to suffer.

As Angela held an envelope that was much thinner than she wished toward their head (and only) journeyman, Davitt looked down at his hands, tightly clenching his hat.

"Pardon me, Mistress."

"What is it, Davitt?"

"If you do not mind a mere journeyman speaking of such matters, I can see your worries over the books. Up-timers do not usually order large monuments, and down-timers have not been ordering them in Grantville. Yes?"

"Yes. And although you are too polite to say it, my husband is not as good at sculpting with the tools we have now as even you, a journeyman, because things were different up-time." An involuntary sigh escaped. "But what does all this have to do with your Christmas, technically Chanukah, bonus? Take it. You have earned it."

He looked up at her, nudging the envelope slightly closer to her with his fingertip. "But the business needs the money."

"That is our worry, not yours."

Davitt looked at her gently. "Midwinter is no time to be wandering, looking for a new job, and we both know there are no other jobs for a journeyman stone-carver in Grantville right now."

Angela laid the envelope in his hat and squeezed his hand. "All the more reason for you to take your bonus, Davitt. But don't worry so much. We are not quite in such bad shape as all that. We have some things we can sell to keep going until we figure out something new, if we need to. And, as I think everyone knows, our daughter Gabi and her friends in the Barbie Consortium invested well and are richer than Herr Ugolini and I ever imagined being. As much as we don't want to take charity from our high school daughter, of all people, we know we never have to worry about losing the roof over our heads. So please, take the bonus without worries for us."

May 1636

As Angela walked up the hill toward her in-laws' grave, she saw Alberto on the ground in front of it, his tools and tool bag scattered like stone chips on the ground around him. Impatient to finish his father's headstone now that it was warm outside, Alberto had headed up that morning to carve his dad's side.

Angela called out, "Honey, when you didn't come back for lunch, I got worried. Are you okay?"

Alberto shook his head and looked around, eyes a bit glassy and unfocused, face slightly slack, his expression generally a million miles away. "What?"

Sitting down beside him, Angela handed him a thermos of soup, a sandwich, and a bottle of water from her bag. "You missed lunch. I thought you might be hungry, and I was worried. Davitt is minding the shop. Now, eat."

A few minutes later, sandwich crumbs brushed from his lap, Alberto picked up an old chisel, rarely used but *always* in his toolbag, touching the tip with a finger. "I remember using a chisel just like this to open a jar of pickles when I was a kid. Dad was furious. Said I knew better. I did, of course, but I really wanted those pickles. It was as bad as using Mom's fabric scissors on paper. He made me sharpen all the chisels in the shop as punishment."

He smiled fondly. "I never did that again! But after that, he started teaching me how to take care of all the tools. Putting them all back in their place and cleaning up the shop every day became my chore. I was so proud to be 'a big boy' he trusted in the shop, just like our John was when I had him start helping. You remember how mad I was when Dad wouldn't let me work on the big carvings after I dropped out of high school to work for him?"

Angela put her hands on her hips in mock anger. "Remember? How could I forget! You ran off and joined the Army and left me waiting for *three years*! The little bit of German not related to drinking that you picked up while you were stationed in Germany has been a help these last few years. Now, tell me why you are sitting here on the ground with hardly any work done on your father's side of the headstone."

"There's a reason we always took them back to work on. It's damn hard to work at this angle." Deep breath out. "We've both been looking at the books, even before Dad got sick. I've been trying to think of a way to make some money but I'm coming up blank."

"First things first. We're going to go sit under the trees on one of those new benches the Scouts made and have a think while you eat the vegetable soup you're ignoring."

Looking at the benches as they walked toward them, Alberto stopped cold. "Not so new, from the looks of them. The wood isn't holding up well. I'm not sure they're safe to sit on."

"Well then, there's our first idea. See if anyone will pay for stone benches for the cemeteries, downtown, parks, anywhere else they may be needed. Grantville has plenty of people with money now. Surely someone will cough up enough to make it happen."

Alberto's expression lightened but the worry lines were deeply etched. "That doesn't fix the basic problem that people don't need headstones, or footstones, or any other kind of memorial marker, and we simply don't have the skills to compete with the down-time sculptors who have been carving people and fancy designs since they hit puberty."

Angela's laugh tinkled as she punched him playfully. "That's an exaggeration, and you know it. Apprentices aren't allowed to do that kind of work! Davitt has been very clear with you on who should do what, properly speaking. If you say that again, I'll tell him, and you'll get another lecture on who does what in a properly run business, and we both know you don't want that." She tucked her arm back into the space between Alberto's elbow and waist and laid her head on his shoulder as they looked down over the hill toward Route 250, hidden from view by the landscaping. "It's so peaceful. Standing here like this, it's almost like the Ring of Fire never happened."

Alberto leaned his head onto hers, drinking in the peace, letting his mind drift back to Before. "We never did get that trip to Niagara Falls I promised you."

"Niagara Falls is still there."

He laughed. "And so is the Grand Canyon, but Paris and London are a whole lot closer and easier to get to now than either of them."

Eyes twinkling, she grinned. "I'll hold you to that." Alberto's reaction verged on panic. "Oh, don't worry, honey. It's a joke! I don't really expect you to take a homebody like me to Paris or Rome, or anywhere else. You remember how hard it was for you to get me to go to Pittsburgh for the weekend to watch a Steelers game, and I love the Steelers."

"True enough, although I seem to recall the players' tight pants holding more appeal than the actual game." As he hugged her fiercely, Alberto whispered into her hair, "I promise to take you to Paris, London, Rome, and anywhere else you want, as long as I don't have to take a seventeenth-century ship or plane to get there."

Pretending she hadn't heard, Angela pulled back. "Now, I need to get back to the office and you, young man, have a headstone to finish!"

One Week Later

"Mom, Cassie, I need your help. I don't know how much longer we can hang on. There just aren't enough people buying memorials from us. Sure, we get a great commission every now and then, but we need something steady. Do you have any ideas?"

As a bookstore owner, her sister Cassie's mind was one-track. "Have you thought about writing a book?"

Sigh. "Cassie, again, no, we don't know enough about up-time memorials to write a whole book, and down-timers know more than we do about sculpting stone. So, no, we aren't writing a book. Mom?"

"Well, I have had this one idea for a while, but it's a bit out there."

"Bring it."

Carlina Marcantonio walked over to the junk drawer in the big buffet and pulled out an up-time brochure. "Your dad and I talked about maybe buying one of those memorial bricks in Fairmont, but the Ring of Fire happened so we never did."

"Down-timers can make bricks, Mom."

"Don't sass me, young lady, and don't interrupt. No one is telling you to make bricks. Use your eyes and read. It's a fundraiser to buy *engraved* bricks. No reason in the world you can't engrave paving stones instead." Carlina looked smug.

"Huh. But why would people buy them? This says it's a good fundraiser for churches and schools and stuff. We aren't any of those, Mom."

Looking at her like she was three and struggling to figure out why the cat was mad at her for grabbing its tail, Carlina spoke slowly. "You find someone who needs to raise money and they do all the work. You engrave the stones they sell, and you both make money. Then you find another group and do it again. And again, and again, and again."

"That's...not bad. Thanks, Mom. Now to figure out a group who needs to do fundraising."

Cassie said, "The Redbird Institute. It's a new thing I've been hearing about. It's designed to be like this famous place called Chautauqua back up-time. Lots of nature, lots of learning, lots of artistic and technical pursuits, mostly in the summer. Using pavers to create pathways sounds perfect for them. They have finished a few buildings, but they have tons more work and I get the feeling they will be adding onto it for years to come."

"I could kiss you both! But I'll ask Gabi to send you some good coffee instead. What? Don't look at me that way. She can afford it, and she likes to do nice things for us. I just hope she doesn't decide that my asking for some coffee means she and the rest of the Barbie Consortium should build an entire eco-friendly coffee plantation or something crazy like that." She shook the cobwebs out. "Well, if they do, we'll for sure get good coffee going forward, so I won't worry about it. The Barbies are clearly good with their money. I'm going to go talk to Alberto right now. Can I take this brochure, Mom? Thanks! You two are lifesavers."

As the door banged behind her, she could hear her mom calling, "That's what family is for, dear!"

* * *

Angela waited until Alberto took a break to bring up the subject. "Do you remember before we came to Germany the diocese in Fairmont was talking about some kind of memory bricks as a fundraiser?"

"Oh, yeah. I forgot about that. You could pay to have a brick engraved with a name or whatever, and they would put it in the new patio. For a little more money, the company could make a small version to keep at home, but everyone thought that was a stupid waste of money, because it was. I wonder how that turned out?"

"It doesn't matter how it turned out! We could do that here. Don't you see? Instead of bricks, we engrave paving stones. We can get all the up-timers to buy bricks, paving stones, for the people they left behind! With all the people moving out of town, at least some of them will probably buy those stupid, waste-of-money small versions."

Alberto shrugged. "It's a good short-term infusion of cash, but it doesn't solve our bigger problem. Down-timers either aren't interested in what we do, or they can afford someone more skilled. Besides, there are only so many people who were left up-time."

Angela left out a deep breath as she counted to ten. *He can be so thick sometimes.* "A lot of down-timers like to do things up-timers do. Not all of them, but enough. It's *très chic* to mimic us. If we can get the up-timers buying carved paving stones, then we can get down-timers to copy them. If we play our cards right, we may be able to convince down-timers of moderate means to buy carved paving stones for their loved ones' graves. It will be a lot cheaper than a full-on headstone and they can always take it home whenever the body is eventually disinterred."

Alberto's eyes widened, and she could see the energy coming back to him and some of his depression lightening. Hope is an amazing tonic. "You're right!" He picked up his wife, kissing her and twirling around the office. "This just may be the ticket! It will buy us breathing room to get more apprentices and journeymen and a bigger office and..."

"Hold on there, let's not get too far ahead of ourselves. I like this office just fine! I'll admit, I wouldn't say no to adding a second floor for the apprentices and such to live in, maybe some more workspace out back, better soundproofing. Okay. Let's go ahead and get ahead of ourselves for just a little while! Then we'll be back to figuring out how to convince the Redbird Institute this is a good idea."

Alberto stopped and put her down, just as fast as if they were playing a very competitive game of musical chairs and the music had stopped. "What do you mean Redbird Institute? Who are they?"

"Did I forget? Right. It's a new idea for a summer art-and-learning institute being built out past Rudolstadt. There will be activity year-round, but mostly it will be almost a summer camp and intellectual salon combined for adults. Since they will be building it for a few years and it will have a lot of outside areas, the Redbird Institute seems like an ideal area to pitch the idea of buying memorial stones. We can have one path or patio or whatever for people left up-time, and another for anyone else." Wanting to give her beloved even more hope, she added, "Maybe we could get them buying stones for people who will never exist now, like George Washington or Marie Curie or Mark Twain, and people we want to remember who didn't live in Grantville, like church friends in Fairmont."

Grinning again, Alberto kissed his wife on the tip of her nose and, humming his favorite Garth Brooks tune, went back to work.

June 1636

As Cassie told her family about how she was helping her sister sell memorial stones for up-timers left behind, her son Ralph had a thoughtful look. He sopped up the last of his (surprisingly tasty) turnip and lentil soup with oven-fresh bread and wiped his mouth. "Mom, right when we came back here, we, you, were working on my Eagle Court of Honor. Half the people you said I should thank were left up-time. I can't remember how many times over the last few years I wished Mr. Jones was here. All that stuff he taught our Explorer Post, and he was so into the Civil Air Patrol. All those books he had on trains and military history, and state Department of Transportation stories from when he worked there. I bet there's a ton he could've helped us with."

Everyone around the dinner table nodded his or her agreement. Bob Jones wasn't the shy and retiring type. They had all talked to him more than a few times over the years.

Cassie nodded her agreement. "I can just hear him telling down-timers about working as a brakeman at the Enola trainyards and how they were the biggest in the world, bigger than anything in West Virginia. I can hardly believe how enormous that place was, and I saw pictures. Down-timers would think he was just pulling their leg."

Ralph's father, Matt, smiled. "Or how he got shipped the whole way to Europe as a combat medic right after basic training when he told a sergeant he was full of it. Didn't know a thing about combat medicine and got sick as a dog on the boat, but he made lifelong friends in Liverpool and saw the Beatles live before they were famous."

Ralph smiled too. Bob had that effect on people. "Mr. Jones was a real dog person. He always seemed to have a collie with him when we went hiking or camping. My favorite story was when he came home from Scout summer camp with a mohawk, and his mom made him go to church that way. So, what do you think if I buy one of these memorial stones for him?"

A tear slipped out as his mother replied, "I think that would be just perfect, kiddo. We can go over and set it up tomorrow morning, before your leave is over."

The Redbird Institute
May 1637

As they watched the workers, Angela squeezed Cassie's hand. "I wish Ralph could've been here to see this."

Cassie nodded. "It meant a lot to him. After he dropped the money for the stone off with you, he came home and told us it was the very first one you sold. I don't think he really believed it would also be the first one installed, but we are sending him a copy of the *Grantville Times* article on it, so he'll know."

"I already talked to Jacob Fiedler. He's taking the pictures for the *Times*, as usual, and he's sending us a set of prints for Ralph, so he'll have nice clear copies of all the pictures." Cobblestone paths weren't exactly an innovation, so things normally went fast, but normally the workers didn't need to read and carefully place each stone so it could be read and found easily. Having an expensive memorial stone placed with the engraving against the dirt, invisible, would be an embarrassing mistake. Once those were all installed, the rest had to be placed "temporarily." That might mean weeks, or it might mean years. But at some point, they might be removed to add in a memorial stone. All of which meant they couldn't be installed in the usual way, which was a headache and meant the workers were cranky.

"Cassie, I'm funned out with this. Let's go sit and enjoy the lake view before we head back to town. Did I ever tell you about my conversation with Ralph when he came in to buy the stone?" At her sister's head shake, Angela continued, "Well, I was confused. Matt's parents were Ralph's only close family I could think of who were left behind, and I figured Matt would buy stones for them, if you wanted to.

"When I asked who he was buying a stone for, he told me it was his favorite Scout leader, Mr. Jones. If it wasn't for him, he wouldn't have earned Eagle, and he said he didn't think Mr. Jones knew that Ralph realized how much Mr. Jones had helped him. You would have been so proud of him. He admitted that he probably didn't realize it five years ago, but now he wants to make sure that Mr. Jones is remembered in our new timeline. 'He loved Scouts. He was proud of being an Army vet, and he always bragged about his wife and kids. So, here you go. One filled out form, thankfully not in triplicate, and payment in full.' Ralph was so proud to be doing something to make sure his Scout leader, left behind, is not forgotten.

"So here it is. Our very first memorial stone, in memory of a man who was clearly loved and admired by many. May he rest in peace."

Robert L. K. Jones

Scout Soldier

Husband & Dad

1935 - RoF

A Meeting at Midsummer, Part 2

Marc Tyrrell

S ee *Eric Flint's 1632 & Beyond* Issue 2 for "A Meeting at Midsummer, Part 1."

Hilltop off West Main Street
Saturday, June 21, 1631, 9:20 p.m.

From the hilltop where Paul sat, he could see the lights of Grantville spread out below him. An hour ago, he had kindled a small fire using an optical glass—a need fire—which he would use as a meditative device once the sun had fully set and the last of the twilight was gone. He would stay here until the sun rose.

He had already cast his circle and set up wards, with small dish candles marking each Quarter. Glancing once more at the sky, he figured that he should start now.

"*Ateh, Malkuth, Ve Geburah, Ve Gedulah, Le Olam, amen.*" Like many Alexandrians, Paul was a firm believer in the doctrine of "If it works, use it. If it doesn't, pitch it." He saw nothing wrong with using a Kabbalistic prayer, since it worked for him. Chrystal had done things differently.

By the end of the prayer, he could feel himself touching the energies of the circle and, beyond it, of the sky and land. His sense of time was already shifting as he stared into the need fire.

"Show me what I need to do."

Paul felt his vision both narrowing and extending, as if he were staring through a magnifying glass. The flames swirled in what seemed to be random patterns but, slowly, started to resolve into an image. He could not really make out what he was seeing, but it looked something like a burning staff, or maybe a spear. He felt tugged towards it, but had no sense of where it might be.

"Where?" He thought he spoke aloud, but it might have only been in his head. The flames shifted and seemed to lose all pattern. Normally, when he used a fire for divination, Paul would keep his focus locked on the flames. But now, for some reason, he felt his head rise up until he was looking at the now dark sky, just beginning to show stars.

Something moved in the sky. He could not make out what it was, but it seemed to be a point of light—no, two of them—moving to the north. He felt drawn that way and, for an instant, he saw what might have been the image of a man holding a long spear. Or it might have been an image supplied by his subconscious; he had no way to tell. The image cut off and his head came down, vision swirling as if he was having an attack of vertigo. His body snapped backwards away from the fire. Once his vision refocused, all he saw were stars that seemed to flow, drawing him out of his trance and back to his fire.

"Hello, the fire!"

Paul tried to sit up as he heard the voice. Vaguely, he could make out the silhouette of a man standing about twenty feet north of him, maybe ten feet from the boundary of his circle.

"Mind if I join you, lad?" the voice asked with a hint of laughter running beneath it. Normally, Paul would have been frightened if someone found him in a circle. After all, West Virginia wasn't exactly the most welcoming place for Wiccans. But for some reason, he did not feel threatened.

"Ah, sure. Come on over." Paul concentrated on opening the circle as the figure walked through and then closing it behind him. "Pull up a rock and join me."

Paul looked at the man and wondered who he was. He was dressed like a down-timer—tunic, pants, cloak and a floppy hat—but he also spoke quite understandable, even colloquial, English. "Can I offer you some wine?" Paul asked as he gestured to his chalice that already had wine in it. *WTF? I can't believe I'm doing this!*

"Why, thank you lad! I hadn't expected a guesting cup! Might I share some bread and salt with you in return?" The man reached into a pouch on his right side and pulled out a loaf of bread and a small twist of cloth. *Bread and salt. The traditional signs of hospitality; guest-right and truce. Weird!* Paul thought.

"I would be honored, sir." Paul watched as the old man pulled two large chunks of bread off the loaf and sprinkled salt on them. Paul took one, ate a bite of it and then drank from the chalice before handing it over. He saw the man nod in approval, take a bite from his own bread and follow it with a sip of wine.

"Ah, now that we have that done and are at peace, can you tell me what you are doing up here? I saw the need fire and was intrigued, since most of your folk don't seem to follow the Old Ways. I certainly don't see many other fires on the hilltops tonight!" The man leaned back and looked at Paul.

"I needed to clear my mind and try to see where I would be going, sir." Paul wasn't sure why he kept calling this man "sir", but it felt right. "Ever since we got here, I have felt off balance. In 'survival mode' you might say, with no sense of purpose. I needed to regain my sense of purpose."

"And have you, lad?" The man cocked his head, and Paul could see the firelight reflected off of his eyes.

"I...don't know." Paul shook his head, trying to order his thoughts. "I have a...feeling? that I need to be going north of here and...meet? someone." He saw the old man nod his head. "I have no idea, though, what I'm supposed to do there. This just seems like minute-to-minute 'purpose,' not something that I can hold onto for a longer period of time."

"Maybe knowing a longer purpose would interfere with what you need to actually achieve it. Sometimes, lad, knowledge of your future can interfere with you achieving your *wyrd*." He paused. "So, you will be going north?"

"I...yes, I will be."

"Good! Maybe you will run into a relative of mine. He goes by the name of Heinrich Förster nowadays. I've heard that he had to flee his home in the Harz mountains due to Tilly's raiders. If you happen to run into him on your journey, say 'hello' for me."

"I'll do that, sir. Oh, wait, I don't know your name."

"Call me Gagnrad. It's as good as anything else I'm known by. Heinrich will know who I am by that name."

"And I'm Paul, Gagnrad. Pleased to meet you."

Gagnrad smiled. "And good to meet you too, Paul, although that name doesn't really suit you. You strike me as more of a Glapsvin than anything else." Gangrad's smile got even larger. "Then again, one never knows! I'll gift you that name, without let or hindrance. And now, unfortunately, I must be off. I have a ways to go this night. *Was hail!*" Gagnrad stood up and walked through the circle as if it wasn't there.

"*Gif hail!*" Paul called after him as he walked out of sight.

Slate Lane
Sunday, June 22, 1631, 5:40 a.m.

Paul walked back to the house on Slate Lane in somewhat of a quandary. He knew what he needed to do, but he still wasn't sure if everything last night hadn't been an illusion. *Still*, he thought, *at least I have an immediate goal, whether it's real or not, and we really do need better intelligence on troop movements in the north.*

As Paul walked up to the house, he could hear Gertrude singing a hymn: *Ein Feste Burg.* Paul hummed along, thinking the words in English. It really was a catchy tune, even if he disagreed with the words. *Then again*—he snorted—*it's not like the neo-pagan movement came up with anything better! A minor, D minor...* Paul laughed, once again recognizing that Wicca had yet to produce any really good composers.

"*Guten morgen,* Gertrude! Martin. Is Hamish here?" Paul called out as he entered the kitchen.

Martin looked at him and nodded. "*Ja,* he came back late from the Thuringen Gardens and is still sleeping. And on the Sabbath! I will wake him up soon, so he can go to church, even if it is that heathen Calvinist church." Martin and Gertrude were staunch Lutherans.

"Don't worry, Martin. I'll wake him up now. I have something that we need to do today, and he is going to have to do most of the organizing." Paul spoke with an increasingly evil grin. He maintained the grin as he left the kitchen and went upstairs to the bunk room where Hamish was sleeping.

Even before he reached the second floor, he could hear Hamish's snores. *How can such a small man produce such a huge noise?* Paul wondered. Opening the door to the bunk room merely increased the volume. Paul felt no worries whatsoever when he grabbed the pitcher of water on the table and threw it on Hamish's face.

"Wake up you slug-a-bed!" Hamish sat up quickly, twisting to reach for his sword which was not available, and smacking his head into the top bunk. "Ow! God's Blood! What are ye doing ye bloody Sassenach! Oh, my broken head!"

"Get off your arse, Hamish. We have a recon mission to run. You've got a choice: go out on the mission with me or spend your time explaining to Reverend Wiley why you look like death warmed over. You've got two minutes, which is when I expect to see you in the kitchen, to decide." Paul turned around and left the room, heading back downstairs to the kitchen.

"Martin," Paul said as he walked into the kitchen "can you ask Gertrude to get together enough travel food for two people for seven days? Hamish and I are going out on a mission." Martin nodded and talked with Gertrude, who started putting together food.

Hamish walked into the kitchen. His eyes, what anyone could see of them, were bloodshot. "Is there at least something to take away this pounding in my head?" he asked plaintively.

"Here, have some coffee. That should help." Paul passed him a mug, and Hamish went over to the table and ladled in three heaping teaspoons of sugar. "Ahhhh."

Paul snorted as he got his own coffee: black, no sugar. "Gertrude is putting together food for us. We're going out on a recon patrol." Paul said as he looked Hamish in the eyes.

Hamish nodded. "A there-and-back?"

"No. We're out for at least four days, possibly a week. I have intel that says we need to meet up with someone soon, but I'm not sure where. You need to get the horses ready."

Hamish looked at Paul. "Horses, is it? And since when could you ride at more than a walk, boyo?"

"Needs must, Hamish. I may not be a great rider, but I can stay in the saddle."

It was Hamish's turn to snort. Paul on a horse resembled a sack of grain. It was a bit of a running joke between them. "Fine, then. On your head, and arse, be it!"

"Just go get them. I'll get my kit together and be waiting for you out front in, say, half an hour."

North of Grantville
Sunday, June 22, 1631, 12:45 p.m.

Paul and Hamish rode through the hills to the north of Rudolstadt towards the crossroads at Teichel. Hamish's hangover seemed to be gone. Coffee, and several up-time aspirins, had done their job.

"Well, will you look at that, Paul! 'Tis a beautiful day, even if I was woken up by a screaming Sassenach before the day ere began!" Hamish's good humor was, occasionally, hard for Paul to bear. Of course, Paul had been up for over twenty-four hours and was still trying to process what had happened the night before. And he was on horseback, never his favorite place.

"Let's stop at Kranichfeld, Hamish. I want to talk with the town guard there and see what they are hearing. We can leave later in the afternoon and make it to Nauendorf in time for dinner."

"What are ye looking for, Paul?"

Paul rode on in silence for a moment. "Mainly information, but I've been told that I might meet someone who can give us something more."

Hamish looked at him questioningly.

"Fine, I have been told that a particular man, one Heinrich Förster, will be able to give us pretty detailed information going back into the Harz mountains. We need that intel, Hamish." Paul put a mental push on the last statement, willing that Hamish would agree.

"From the Harz mountains, ye say? Aye, that would be useful, especially if he can give us any idea of where that bastard Tilly's troops are! He's one o' yours?" Hamish's question hung in the air.

"No. He's a relative of an acquaintance of mine, who asked me to look out for him. It could be important."

Niederzimmen, between Erfurt and Weimar
Sunday, June 22, 1631, 4:35 p.m.

"Come on, we have to move. Now!" Heinrich spoke forcefully to the three women who were with him. Birgitte and Anna moved carefully forward through the field, while Magdalena limped after them. Heinrich followed behind holding the spear at the ready.

One mile north of Niederzimmen, between Erfurt and Weimar
Sunday, June 22, 1631, 5:15 p.m.

"Keep moving, Captain." Father Salazar's voice was harsh. "We need to find those witches and send them back to Hell. Don't forget, they killed at least five men in our camp. The Holy Father wants you to catch them and, if you don't, you will answer for it!"

Captain Theodosius von Thieren looked at Salazar and wondered, for about the tenth time, why he had taken Tilly's coin. Yes, it was important that the emperor's writ covered the entire empire, but did that mean that he had to put up with this carping jackass in a dress?

"We have to wait for the tracker, Father," he said in a calm voice. *As if I hadn't already told you that, you slack-witted turd!* he thought. "Soon enough, we will pick up their trail again and find them." He turned and looked at the tracker coming towards them.

"What do you say, Johan?" von Thieren asked.

"They came this way, my lord. They appear to be heading for the village south of us."

Von Thieren nodded. "Fine. Mount up, and let's go there. Remember"—he raised his voice to the other men in the group—"we don't have the force to take anything. Our mission is to capture the witches. Any man who gets out of line will be dealt with."

One mile south of Mőnchenholthausen
Sunday, June 22, 1631, 5:35 p.m.

"We need to get into the hills. The forest cover should shield us. It won't be dark for another four hours or so, so we should be able to find our way through the woods to the other side."

Heinrich was starting to feel a little desperate. Yes, he had rescued the Spear and three of the women, but he was being tracked by that damned priest, Odin's curse be on him!

Niederzimmen, between Erfurt and Weimar
Sunday, June 22, 1631, 5:45 p.m.

"We are seeking the whereabouts of four witches." Von Thieren's voice rang out in the village square. "We know that they came near here and that you, the righteous people of Niederzimmen, would never harbor them."

Father Salazar's face looked like he had sucked a lemon, but he said nothing.

The few villagers in the open looked at each other in confusion. "There ain't no witches here, Captain! We drove them away with the fires last night!" one yelled.

"Ah, yes, the midsummer fires. Well done, my good man!"

The villager looked at von Thieren as if he couldn't quite believe what he had heard.

"So," von Thieren continued, "it is obvious to me, and to the Holy Father here of course, that the inhabitants of Niederzimmen reject the Devil and all his works." He watched as the villagers nodded.

"And I am sure that you wish to see any witches we might find executed. For I tell you, we are tracking four witches who have killed at least five brave defenders of Christ." Von Thieren sent up a prayer of thanksgiving for his early schooling in rhetoric. Otherwise, he would not have been able to say what he had just said with a straight face, given who had actually died.

"Have any of you seen these four witches? We believe that they are one man carrying a spear, and three women."

The villagers looked at each other, until one spoke up. "Aye, sir. I saw four people—one man and three women—heading south 'bout an hour gone. The man, he was carrying what looked like a long spear."

"South, you say?"

"Aye, sir, aimin' at Mŏnchenholthausen or thereabouts. Maybe Klet-tbach on the Rudolstadt road. We hear that there's some kind of town full of witches and wizards that appeared near there."

"Thank you, my good man." Von Thieren flipped him a silver *pfennig.* "We have need of food and drink. Might your village be able to provide for us before we must leave?"

Black Tree Inn, Nauendorf
Sunday, June 22, 1631, 5:55 p.m.

"My ass feels like I've been kicked by a bull!" In truth, Paul was having a hard time of it.

Hamish just laughed. "I'll just go get us a meal and a room then, while the lad here takes care of our horses."

Hamish pulled off his saddlebags and handed the reins to the young boy. Hamish walked to the door of the Black Tree Inn with Paul following behind with his own saddlebags and rifle.

"Sit yerself down, Paul."

Paul just nodded and sat at an empty table. Soon enough, two steins of beer appeared, brought by a bar maid. Hamish finished talking with the inn's owner and rejoined Paul.

"Well, we have a room an' a meal soon. Grab yer stein and haul yerself out of the chair and let's eat outside. You'll be needing to walk around a mite so that ye don't stiffen up like a corpse."

Paul reluctantly got out of his chair, gathered his saddlebags, gun, and stein and tottered after Hamish. He could see several tables with benches and hear a small brook tinkling in the background.

Dropping his saddlebags and propping his gun up on the bench next to him, Paul sat down again and took a long pull from his stein. "Ah, now that hits the spot!"

"True, that. Much better than the piss water you folks brought with you." Hamish took a long pull from his stein as well. "In truth, Paul, yer doin' well for a mon that doesna ride. I had no expected we'd get this far in one day."

Paul nodded. "I hadn't either, really. I'm going to crash after dinner though, since we should probably get up at dawn. I'd like to try to get closer to Erfurt to see what's going on over there. From what I could see on the map, there's really only a couple of routes for Tilly's troops to hit us in any large number, and those mainly bypass Erfurt to the south."

Hamish nodded. "Aye, ye've the right of that. They could also bring at least a tercio down this road to try and hit Rudolstadt, but there's not much here for them to live off. More likely to bypass Erfurt, drop down towards Stadtilm and Badenburg. Lots of farms thataway to feed the bastards."

A wooden platter with bread, cheese and sliced meats landed in front of each of them. "*Mehr bier, meine herren?*"

Paul nodded and Hamish replied, "*Ja, danke. Einen krug, bitte.*" The barmaid nodded, smiled, and went back inside.

Two miles south of Mönchenholthausen
Sunday, June 22, 1631, 8:45 p.m.

"Well, sir, it looks like that last peasant we talked with was right. They came this way."

"Are you certain, Johan?" von Thieren asked.

"Aye, sir. If you look here carefully, you can see the footprint of one of the women. It's unbalanced, and probably means that she strained her ankle. We know that one of the women had that problem back at the camp, so I would say it's pretty certain this is the group we're looking for."

Von Thieren nodded. "Right. Where do you think they are going now, Johan?"

"I don't really know this area, sir, but from what little I've gotten from the locals, the path here splits, with the southern part going to some place called Klettbach on the Rudolstadt road, and one part going east to a place called Berka. The hills are also pretty heavily forested, so they may be going in here just to hide."

"So, what do you think of our chances of catching them, given the remaining light?"

"Well, sir, I think it would take God's own miracle to do that. As soon as we go up this slope"—Johan pointed due south up the trail—"the light gets blocked by the trees, and everything is shadowed. I won't be able to tell if they have turned off the trail and gone into the woods. We could blunder around for hours without finding anything."

"All right, Johan, we stop here for the night. I want us up with the dawn, though. And set a watch."

In the hills above Klettbach
Sunday, June 22, 1631, 9:05 p.m.

"Heinrich!" Birgitte's whisper was forceful but, hopefully, couldn't be heard for more than a few feet. "Magdalena can't go any farther, and I'm not sure how much longer Anna and I can stay awake. We have got to rest."

"All right, let's get settled in for the night. There's still a little bread left, and we have a full waterskin. We'll sleep here and start moving before dawn."

Two miles south of Mőnchenholthausen
Monday, June 23, 1631, 4:45 a.m.

Theodosius von Thieren found himself sitting in an inn, talking with his sister. Which was odd since, to the best of his knowledge, Mathilde had never gone to an inn, let alone drunk beer in one. It was odder still since she had also died in childbirth four years past, but that didn't seem to stop her from taking a large mouthful.

"So," Mathilde looked at him as she placed her stein on the table. "why did you do it?"

"Do what, sister?"

"Don't be an idiot, brother mine!" Mathilda's eyes were furrowed in a frown he knew well. "Why did you follow the orders of the Hound?"

"You mean Father Salazar?"

"Well what other rabid Hound is around you right now? Of course I mean that disgusting excuse for a human being! So, why did you do it?"

Von Thieren shrugged. "He's a priest and an inquisitor. He ordered me to come with him. It is my duty to God to follow his priests."

Mathilde's gaze made him shrink. "Really? So if some drunken fool in a bedsheet tells you to jump off a cliff, you would do it? You do realize, I hope, that this Salazar is about as much a true priest as what you shat out your butt yesterday." That was Mathilde—always blunt. He had missed talking with her.

"Listen, brother mine, you still have a chance to make good on your mistake. Oh, and by the way, if you get Johan killed, I will be really mad at you! He was our playmate growing up, and you owe him a duty that, at the moment, you are not fulfilling. Make sure that you fix it."

"Wake up, sir!" von Thieren felt a hand on his shoulder and rolled over. The, yes, it must have been a dream of Mathilde and the inn fading into the light of pre-dawn. Johan was waiting for him. "It's just before dawn, sir. We should be able to see well enough in about twenty minutes."

"Thank you, Johan." Von Thieren looked around the camp to see who else was up. No one seemed to be stirring, and he couldn't see any sentries. "What happened to the watch?"

"They fell asleep, sometime. I woke up about an hour ago, and their fire had burned down to embers. I think they were drunk."

"Stupid fools! Don't they...*scheiß*, no they probably don't realize that we could have all had our throats slit last night. I'm beginning to think that for this lot, it would be an improvement! Let's get them up and get started."

In the hills above Klettbach
Monday, June 23, 1631, 5:25 a.m.

Heinrich snapped awake. Quickly glancing at the sky, he realized that he had overslept, and day was fully upon them.

"Birgitte, Anna, Magdalena." He grabbed each shoulder in turn and shook it. "It's after dawn, and we have to move."

Quickly, the women gathered what little they had while Heinrich made sure of the waterskin and the spear. He looked carefully at the terrain and decided that they had to avoid coming near the village below them. There was a small stream flowing south from the village with what looked like a road near it. Over to his left, the land dipped down into a small valley that appeared to lead to the road.

Right, he thought, *that's the way we have to go. We can stay in the woods until we're out of sight of the village.*

Black Tree Inn, Nauendorf
Monday, June 23, 1631, 6:10 a.m.

Paul felt both stiff and rested. A curious combination, he would admit, but most of all, he felt alive as he and Hamish rode away from the Black Tree Inn at a sedate walk along the Rudolstadt road leading to Erfurt.

"Another day, ye figure, Paul?"

"Probably, Hamish. At least another day out and then, if we don't find anything, we'll head back."

Half a mile south-east of Klettbach
Monday, June 23, 1631, 6:12 a.m.

Heinrich and the women had stopped to rest for a couple of minutes after scrambling down the valley towards the tree line next to the small creek. The road ran for maybe five hundred yards on the other side of the creek before crossing a bridge. If Heinrich was reading things correctly, they would be out of sight from the village once they were past the bridge.

"Let's go. We need to stay on this side of the stream and join up with the road where the bridge crosses."

In the hills above Klettbach
Monday, June 23, 1631, 6:18 a.m.

"I have to say, Captain, that I am impressed with your tracker! To have found where they stayed last night so quickly. Maybe I should take him with me." Salazar was smiling in a manner that would have been more becoming to a painting of Mephistopheles.

"Johan is a treasure, yes. His family has served mine for over two hundred years." Von Thieren looked around and could easily tell where four people had burrowed into the underbrush to sleep. He knew that they couldn't have been gone for long, but that knowledge did not lighten his spirits.

"Look, down there in the tree line, moving towards that bridge!" One of Salazar's thugs, von Thieren didn't want to know his name, called out. "Mount up and get after them!"

"Stop!" von Thieren cried out before he realized what he was doing. "Are you fools? Do you want to die? Do you want your horses to die? You can't take a horse down that slope. We need to backtrack and pick up the trail to that little village down there with the road running through it." He suited actions to words and turned his horse back towards the path they had followed up here.

"Johan, hold up!" he called.

Johan looked up at him with a question in his eyes as Salazar's men rode past him towards the path.

"Relax, and let's just walk our horses to the path and down to the road. Let Salazar's goons go ahead."

"I, ah, take it then, sir, that you don't mind missing out on the capture?" One of Johan's eyebrows was slightly raised.

"I think it may be time for Niemand to be here, rather than me. I will see you in a little while."

Niemand, or "no man" was a shared joke. As boys growing up together, they had thrilled to read Homer's Odyssey, and von Thieren had been particularly taken by the story of Odysseus and the Cyclops. Ever since they heard it, whenever von Thieren wanted to talk with Johan with no barriers of rank between them, he became Niemand.

"So what are you really thinking, Niemand?" Johan asked with a slight smile on his face. It had been quite some time, over a year in fact, since they had talked like this.

"Salazar is a pig, a fanatic, and a disgrace to his priesthood. He sickens me, and I can only apologize for having brought you in on this." Von Thieren hung his head. "What is worse, I think he is insane, maybe possessed, with his rantings about witches."

"Possessed? Maybe. He is definitely a fanatic and, perhaps, as you say, insane. Why do you really think we're here?"

"Honestly? I have no fucking idea. I think that crazy bastard feels he can take anything he wants and use it to achieve any end he has in mind. Yes, I did agree that we needed to track down the people who killed our soldiers. We can't let that go without punishment.

"At the same time, though, look who the missing women were. They were all from one place, and I suspect that the man who is with them followed them here to rescue them. Were they our men who were killed? No, they were with Salazar and Schirmer, and I don't doubt that they committed all of the usual atrocities!" Von Thieren's voice was filled with loathing. "Which means, Johan, that whoever they are, they are enacting exactly the same justice, rough as it may be, that I would."

"And?"

"And I think I may be on the wrong side. Come on, I hear Captain von Thieren coming back. We should catch up and try to rein in that fanatic Salazar."

Bridge about one mile south of Klettbach
Monday, June 23, 1631, 6:40 a.m.

"Come on, Birgitte! Can't you help her to move faster?" Heinrich was starting to get more than a bit desperate. Magdalena's ankle was even worse than it had been yesterday. It was badly swollen, and she could hardly walk without assistance.

He glanced south down the road and could see that there were two people on horseback coming towards them slowly. His head whipped around, and he looked north along the road, hoping that it was empty. It was not. There must have been eight or nine riders pounding down the road towards them. Worse still, Heinrich thought they were soldiers.

"*Scheiß*. Birgitte, you and Anna take Magdalena back into the woods that way." Heinrich was pointing almost due east where the ground rose quickly and was quite wooded. "I'll try and hold them off while you get away."

Fucking ridiculous, he thought, *but, then again, I am Odin's* speerträger. *I've trained for most of my life to use this spear if needed. I guess it's needed now.*

Heinrich walked back to the bridge and stood about six feet from its southern end. The bridge itself was about fourteen feet wide, suitable for heavy wagons. Heinrich held the spear upright, butt on the ground and breathed in a slow, deep breath. *Odin, Geirvaldr, I am already yours. Aid me in sending these murderers to your judgment.* For a moment, he felt totally at peace.

Now, he thought, *let us see how well training works out in actual battle at eight to one odds.* The soldiers were closer now, and he could see several figures lagging behind, one of which was that damned priest. He was not sure about the other two riding behind the priest.

* * *

"Paul, it's Tilly's men!" Hamish reached for his sword and made sure it was loose in its scabbard before checking a couple of truly huge horse pistols.

"Easy, Hamish. Looks like they're after that one guy down by the bridge. There are some women over to the right running up the hill into the woods. I think he's trying to protect them. Damn fool! One against, what, eight? Ten?"

"Eight I think, although it looks like there be another three behind the main body. Well, now, isn't that int'restin'! They're no cavalrymen, ridin' like sacks of barley they are. Worse than you, even!" Hamish's eyes twinkled with that last comment.

"About four hundred yards away, I'd guess. What say we even the odds somewhat?"

"I like tha way yer thinkin', Paul! A quick charge, a round o' shot, then at 'em wi' the sword!"

"Hamish, I hope you remember that I don't have a sword, and I'm not any kind of crazed cavalryman! What I do have is a nice hunting rifle, and I can shoot the head off a squirrel at a hundred yards. You keep right, while I go left. Try and take any of the bastards who go for the women."

* * *

Hans Breitkopf, "Mauler" to his friends, of whom he had very few, was having trouble with his horse. The blasted beast kept running faster and faster, and now Hans was leading the pack as they started across the bridge. He really had no idea what to do when the witch in front of him yelled and thrust out a spear at his horse which, being a silly beast, reared up and threw

Hans off his back and into the bridge railing. The horse kept running as the spearman leapt out of his path.

Hans rebounded from the bridge railing right in front of Gunnar's horse which, after kicking him in the chest, shied to the right and caused Franz's horse to hit the other railing. The others all pulled desperately on their reins trying to stop their beasts and get them under control.

That confusion was all Heinrich needed. Within two seconds, he was back on the bridge. His spear thrust out and caught Hans at the base of the neck. It punched through his spinal cord and dropped him like a marionette with cut strings. Half a second later, the spear was back in Heinrich's hands and starting to twirl as he watched both Gunnar and Franz trying to control their mounts. Two seconds later, the spear blade sliced through Gunnar's throat, before returning to its twirling. Franz started to yell, and the spear blade cut him another mouth.

The horses decided that they had had enough and started retreating. Their riders, or at least those who remained, let them go so they could get off the damn beasts! Some twenty yards back of the north end of the bridge, they managed to get their mounts under control and dismount.

* * *

Paul still had another hundred yards to go when the horsemen pulled back from the bridge, leaving three of their fellows behind. *Damn!* he thought. *That is one serious dude! That spear he has looks like a propeller blade!*

* * *

Heinrich was feeling pretty good. Three down, not a scratch on him, and the bastards were retreating. He took a quick look behind him and frowned. He could see a cavalryman moving towards the women and another rider—maybe a musketeer?—moving to his right. They weren't charging and didn't seem to be directly attacking either him or the women, but they were there and needed to be kept in mind.

He looked back at the priest's men and saw that they had stopped about twenty yards past the bridge to dismount. *Too bad, given how poorly they rode!* He could also see that they were pulling out weapons. Two had pistols, but the rest seemed to have only swords. He went back into his stance, holding the spear upright as he watched them getting ready.

He could see the priest, Salazar, ride up to them and command them to attack. *Freya's tits! That bastard is actually frothing at the mouth! He almost looks like a berserker!* He was intrigued to see the other two riders, one obviously an officer, staying back. For a moment, he seemed to make eye contact with the officer who, he thought, nodded to him.

A quick check behind him, and he saw that the musketeer, or whatever he was, had dismounted almost a hundred yards away. *No danger there,* he thought. The cavalryman also seemed to have halted, although he was somewhat closer, seventy-five yards maybe. The cavalryman actually doffed his hat at him and gave a short bow. *Stranger and stranger,* Heinrich thought.

"Go forth and KILL all of these witches! Burn their bodies! Tear them limb from limb and throw the parts into the fire! Go forth in God's Name and KILL!"

Salazar started to chant.

Dies irae, dies illa.

Heinrich saw his opponents line up with the two pistoleers in front and the three swordsmen behind. They started walking towards him, keeping march time with the chant.

There's something wrong, Heinrich thought as he felt a headache starting. *That's the wrong tune!* Heinrich had heard the proper chant for the *Dies Irae* before, and this definitely was not it.

* * *

A hundred yards away, Paul heard the chant as well, and recognized the words, although not the chant. *What the fuck? That's a spell-song!* Paul had taken part in a really good workshop the previous summer at a festival in New York that dealt with spell-songs. Paul had used that knowledge to write a paper on the use of music in propaganda. It had received the only perfect mark in the class.

Hmm, spell-songs work best on people who are already conditioned to them, which looks like those soldiers. He winced as the priest chanted another tritone. *If that keeps up, I'm going to have a blinding headache soon!* If what he remembered was correct, he knew how to cancel some of the effects of this particular one—if he could only remember the right words!

While Paul was trying to remember the words, the five remaining men had moved to the end of the bridge and started to move toward Heinrich.

* * *

For his part, Heinrich's incipient headache was now firmly established. The priest's chant seemed to echo louder and louder in his brain.

Quantus tremor est futurus.

Heinrich's head was pounding in time with the chant as he watched the two pistoleers raise their weapons and shoot at him. He felt a burning sensation in his right arm and what must have been a mule kicking him in his left leg. He collapsed, banging the back of his head on the floor of the bridge.

Through the mental haze, Heinrich thought he heard a branch snap. The sound of a branch shattered by cold. One of the pistoleers dropped and curled in a ball. *Funny,* Heinrich thought, *it doesn't seem cold.*

Another snap, and the other pistoleer was down as well, clutching his throat. The remaining three men were looking around with confused, glazed, expressions on their faces. But they still maintained their metered march forward, as if the chant controlled them. *And maybe it does,* Heinrich thought as he fought to clear his mind.

Snap!

Snap!

And then there was one. Heinrich did not know it, but the sole remaining man, one Dieter Rilling by name, was not truly evil. He was, however, weak-willed. By this time, he had almost no will left except that of Father Salazar. Prior conditioning, and the chant, had completely overcome him.

In the distance, Heinrich could now hear someone singing. Not well, but loudly. It was a soothing chant, a melody that seemed to counteract what Salazar was chanting. Strangely enough, he recognized the words as being from the same prayer: the *Dies Irae*.

Iudex ergo cum sedebit.

Heinrich shook his head as the priest's final man walked towards him in a daze. He got up, leaning on the spear and hoping his leg wouldn't give out. Heinrich could see the confusion in the other man's eyes as he looked to the right and then the left. Finally, he looked at Heinrich. *"Set me free. Please!"*

There was something in his eyes, perhaps a memory of terror, that spoke to Heinrich's soul. He nodded and slashed the spear so that it cut the man's throat, spraying blood across the bridge and into the stream. He wavered, and his head seemed to nod, then he collapsed and his blood drained out over the bridge. "Go with your gods," Heinrich said.

Salazar had stopped chanting and was staring at Heinrich. "I was wrong." he screamed. "You aren't a witch. You are a demon! How else could you have stopped the power of God's holy song? Demon! I cast you back into the Hell from which you came! Captain!" Salazar turned to the officer behind him. "I command you to kill this demon!"

"You want me to kill the demon, Father Salazar?"

"Yes! Do it NOW!"

Captain von Thieren drew his sword and rode forward holding the blade across his saddle. "As you wish, Father."

As he drew next to Salazar's left, von Thieren moved the sword over his left shoulder and threw a mighty backhand strike toward him. Salazar's head flew off his shoulders and onto the grass.

"There, *Father*. The demon is slain."

He wiped off his sword blade and sheathed it.

"Gentlemen!" Von Thieren's loud voice carried across the field. "I believe we have much to discuss."

Black Tree Inn, Nauendorf
Monday, June 23, 1631, 9:25 p.m.

The sun had gone down behind the hills to the west of Nauendorf, but had not yet set, as Paul sipped at his beer and thought about the day. After the fight at the bridge, and a rather tense discussion as the three groups realized that they were not actually enemies, they had all returned to the Black Tree Inn.

The horses of the fallen had been brought along as well, carrying the bodies of Salazar and his men. Von Thieren and Johan had taken them to the *Dorfkirche* to be buried and then rejoined the rest at the inn. Meanwhile, Hamish had secured rooms and ordered a meal for everyone. They all met outside at two of the tables while they ate. Soon, the women left to rest, while the others talked.

After several hours of discussion, which would have been a lot less if Paul spoke German, Paul thought he understood what had happened and why. Von Thieren had told him that Tilly had ordered his army to disperse and await new orders, which they had mostly done. He also mentioned that he had heard that some of the units, maybe a tercio in size, were going to be marching on Badenburg soon, but that he wouldn't be joining them. When asked why, his response was illuminating.

"I joined this war to maintain the Empire, the Law, and the Church. What I have seen..." he shook his head in disgust. "I really have no words to describe it. Magdeburg was an abomination..." Von Thieren's eyes stared off into space for a moment, then refocused. "I am sorely tempted to just leave and take my men home to Carinthia. At least there we can live like men instead of running with vultures!"

"Would you not take the king of Sweden's colors then?"

"My men and I are Catholic. I doubt that a Lutheran would want us since we won't lie about our faith."

"Ah, well, he's not foolish, and you said you only have, what, fifty men? You could join Captain Mackay and help us to protect people instead of butchering them."

"To what end? To help destroy the Empire?"

"Nae, to help stop the plundering and pillaging and slaughter of innocents! If not Sweden, then perhaps you could join with the Americans. They won't worry about what religion you are. A moment, please, Captain."

Hamish turned to Paul, and translated most of what had just gone on. "Would your folk hire von Thieren and his men?"

"Probably not, Hamish. I don't think we will hire mercenaries as such. That said, if he's worried about being Catholic in Swedish service, we could ask Mackay to base him out of Grantville for a while."

Hamish nodded and translated the offer for von Thieren. "There's a Catholic church in Grantville, so you and your folks could worship freely there. You'd still have to take Swedish colors, but I'm sure Captain Mackay could see clear to have you lodged there, at least for now."

Von Thieren sat back and sipped his beer while he thought. He looked at Johan next to him and raised an eyebrow. Johan shrugged his shoulders.

"All right. I will take the offer to my men. I'm not certain they will accept, and it is not something that I will order them to do. I have"—his mouth assumed a wry grin—"managed to maintain discipline by never giving an order that won't be obeyed."

Hamish, Johan, and Heinrich all laughed, while Paul looked confused. Hamish translated for Paul, who nodded.

Heinrich spoke up. "Captain, there are at least two women from Schierke left in that camp. Can you bring them with you and any others from the village?"

"I will do my best, but I can guarantee nothing."

Heinrich nodded and sighed.

"Johan and I need to head back to our company. I will bring what men wish to come, here, by the thirtieth. Will you have someone here to guide us?"

"Aye, that we will. Probably myself and Paul."

"Good. Johan, we should probably pick up some food for the trip back and leave." Von Thieren stood up, and shook hands with the others, then turned and went into the inn with Johan. Five minutes later, they headed back the way they had come, taking half of the spare horses with them.

"So, Heinrich, what will you and the ladies be doing?" Paul looked at him as Hamish translated. Heinrich thought for a minute, and then spoke.

"We need to get back home, but I don't think we can go back right now. Would we be welcome in Grantville?"

"I don't see why not. We can certainly house you and, if you're willing to work, you should be able to make enough to do well." Paul thought for a moment. "Besides using that spear like a pro, what else can you do?" Paul waited for the translation and response.

"I'm a master blacksmith and bladesmith. If I have access to a forge and iron, I can probably make anything in those lines."

Paul nodded. "So, will you come back with us now? We will be leaving in the morning, but von Thieren left us half the horses, so we can ride."

"Yes, I think that is best."

"By the way, Heinrich, is your last name Förster?"

Heinrich got a questioning look on his face. "Yes, it is. Why?"

"Oh, I ran into a relative of yours by the name of Gagnrad. He said you might be up this way and asked me to keep an eye out for you."

Heinrich's face paled. "He...told you to look for me?"

"He asked, and I said I would. Actually, he asked me to say 'hello' to you if we met."

"Did he say anything else?" Hamish was starting to wonder what was going on, even as he translated.

"Well, just some general talk. Oh, yes, he said that I was more of a Glapsvin than a Paul, and that he would gift me that name." Paul shook his head. "I really have no idea what that was about."

Heinrich snorted. "Yes, I can see that! He can be...difficult to understand sometimes. We will have to talk more once we can speak each other's language."

The rest of the day was spent relaxing and talking. The women joined them for dinner, but everyone except Paul had decided to get an early night. Paul sat in the yard near the stream with the last pitcher of beer, thinking.

"Hello, the inn! Paul, it's good to see you again!"

Paul's head whipped around as he saw an old man in a cape and floppy hat moving towards his table.

"Gagnrad! Good to see you! Come, join me for a beer."

Gagnrad sat down at the table and took a stein, filling it from the pitcher. "So, I see you found Heinrich! Well done, lad! And a good fight it was, too.

I'm sorry about the women, though. Still, the three here are safe for now, and the four left in the camp really couldn't leave."

"Four? Heinrich said he only saw two."

"No, there's four of them left there, but I suspect Captain von Thieren will get them out. He's an interesting man, don't you think, Paul?"

"Ah, yes, sir, I think he is. He is a man of honor, I believe, who fights more for ideals than for gold. I like him."

Gagnrad canted his head and looked at Paul. "But would you trust him at your back, lad?"

Paul thought about that for a moment and then replied. "Yes. If he gave his word, I would trust him almost anywhere and certainly to guard my back."

Gagnrad nodded his head. "That's good to know. It's always well to know if you have someone to guard your back."

Gagnrad leaned back. "So, are Heinrich and the girls going with you?"

"I believe so, at least for now."

"Good." Gagnrad slapped the table. "Excellent, in fact! Paul, I'll ask you to keep an eye on them while they are in Grantville. They won't be able to go home for several months and there are many things that they need to learn."

Paul nodded.

"Two other things if I may, Paul."

Gagnrad was staring at Paul now, which made him feel a bit uncomfortable, but he waved his hand in a "go ahead" motion.

"I believe that Heinrich's foster father is already in Grantville. I wasn't able to see him while I was there, but I am fairly certain he is. His name is Helmut Förster and he is also a blacksmith. Do try to get them together if possible."

Paul nodded. "Of course. I'll see what I can do, but if he's there, I'll try to get the two of them together."

"Thank you, Paul. The final request, if I may, is that one of my relatives still in that camp will need special attention. She is, at the moment, extremely fragile. Her soul is like spun glass hanging in the middle of a cattle stampede. Can you see that she gets the care she needs?"

"I will try, Gagnrad, but that will depend on von Thieren getting her out of the camp and us getting her to Grantville. No promises, except that I will do what I can do as circumstances permit."

"Good, Paul, and thank you. Here, take this as a gift from me." Gagnrad handed Paul a teardrop-shaped red gem on a braided leather necklace.

Paul took the necklace and looked at it carefully. "Carnelian?" he asked.

Gagnrad had a sly, almost mocking, smile on his face. "Aye, that it is, lad. It should help you relax and, maybe, help you with learning German. Well, I need to be off about my business. I am certain we will meet again. *Was hail*!" Gagnrad stood up and raised his right hand before leaving.

"*Gif hail*, Gagnrad!"

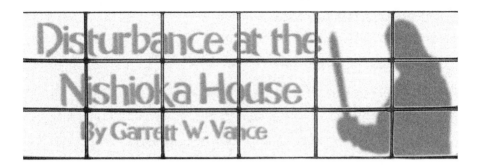

Disturbance at the Nishioka House

Garrett W. Vance

T he second in a three-story series.
See *Eric Flint's 1632 & Beyond* Issue 1 for "Ill-Met in the Marshes."

Phnom Penh docks

The day before

Blom Corneliszoon leaned on the rail of his ship *Groenevisch* as he watched a small army of dockworkers load cargo aboard. He had done well this trip, very well, and a sense of relief filled him, along with a deep satisfaction. This was his first solo trip to Asia as captain, and he had pulled it off with style and aplomb. His uncles were nearby, of course, captaining the other family ships, *Vlissengen Tuin* and *Groote Hoop* that were docked just down the quay from him. He knew they kept their sharp eyes on him, but he didn't mind. Despite their usually dour demeanor, they were always good to him. Now they gave him a free hand, allowing him to command *Groenevisch* throughout the voyage on his own. It was good to be at sea again. Blom had spent a few years working as a trader back in Ayutthaya, but ultimately the sedentary life hadn't agreed with him. The thrill of travel, with all its perils and wonders, was the life for him!

Something nudged his elbow. He looked down to find the ship's cat, Nebuchadnezzar, taking a stroll along the rail. Nebuchadnezzar was a very large fellow of Siamese heritage. He had the famous, or in some people's opinion, *infamous* pantherine look, but lacked the boisterous temperament, preferring to maintain a low profile. His thick, smooth fur was a rich chocolate brown, and his eyes a striking chartreuse. Interestingly, the so-called "Siamese" cats he had encountered in Grantville were quite different, with bat-like ears and blue eyes. The proud owner had explained to him that this was the result of several centuries of selective breeding, and that cats like Nebuchadnezzar, who were the modern version's ancestors, were now considered to be a different breed altogether. It all seemed like much ado about nothing to Blom, but it was yet another indication of the sometimes subtle changes the long passage of time had wrought.

Nebuchadnezzar had showed up on *Groenevisch* when they were docked in Ayutthaya, uninvited of course, as cats tend to do, making his presence known by depositing a very large, very dead rat, almost as big as the roughly six-month-old kitten himself, at Blom's feet. He then stared up at Blom until the kindly captain reached down and gave him a pat on his head, which he silently tolerated.

"Well now, welcome aboard, young sir! It seems you are applying for the position of *Master Mouser* here on *Groenevisch*. I can see you know how to earn your keep, so you have the job. My congratulations! Now, what shall I call you? Brownie? Green Eyes?"

Before Blom could decide, the newest member of the crew picked up his prize and sauntered away with a regal gait, his goal having been accomplished he did not require any further small talk.

"Ah, a king among cats it would seem! In that case, I shall call you Nebuchadnezzar, a rather extravagant name perhaps, but befitting such a majestic example of the feline species as yourself!"

And so, Nebuchadnezzar became the ship's cat, pursuing his rodent-slaying commission with relentless determination. He was never affectionate, enduring the occasional pat from Blom and the crew with long-suffering patience until he could slip away into the shadowy realm below decks that was his solemn charge and kingdom.

Growing weary of the captain's lengthy reminiscences, Nebuchadnezzar gave Blom another nudge, then stared at him expectantly with his large, luminous eyes.

"Oh! I see! I am in your way. How rude of me!" Blom withdrew his arms from the rail, opening the way for Nebuchadnezzar to pass. Head held high, the venerable cat, no longer a kitten after several years of service, but grown into something approaching the size of the wild panthers he so very much resembled, continued his patrol. Blom made a point of giving his plush coat a gentle stroke as he went by, just to remind the haughty fellow who the master of this ship really was. Nebuchadnezzar allowed himself a brief acknowledgment of the attention with an arch of his long back and a rumbling purr, then continued on his way.

"Strange old cat, aren't you?" Blom muttered after him. Nebuchadnezzar's brief visit served to break his reverie; it was time to go do something—but what?

It was late afternoon, and *Groenevisch's* remaining business for the day was in the capable hands of his first mate Mijnheer van Zijl, a most dependable fellow indeed. So, how should he occupy the hours ahead? Just then he heard a low rumbling reminiscent of Nebuchadnezzar's vibrating purrs. His stomach was growling!

"Ah! Time to eat!" As far as Blom was concerned, *any* time was time to eat; it was by far his dearest pastime. Blom was a firm devotee of fine meals and a full belly. With a rueful grin, he hitched up his belt, which was partially hidden beneath a fairly substantial roll of fat, a bit more than a man of his thirty-one years might prefer to carry, but not too heavy a price to pay for the satisfaction his never-ending pursuit of fine food provided him.

Now, where to go? His favorite meals by far were the fabulous Japanese *bento* lunches his dear friend Yoriaki's wife Momo made, but Nihonmachi was a longish, dusty ride from the docks, and they were undoubtedly busy packing for the journey ahead. No, he would have to make do with something closer. He considered his options for a moment while twirling the waxed end of his gracefully curving mustache, as was his habit when deep in thought.

"Ah ha! I know just the place!" he exclaimed to himself. With first a quick word to Mijnheer van Zijl as to his intended whereabouts in case his presence was required, Blom bounced down one of the gangplanks, which definitely sagged a bit with each heavy step.

Blom sauntered down the pier looking as if all the world was his oyster, and he had just sharpened his shucking knife. Not only was he on his way to a fine meal, but things were good today, *very* good, splendid in fact. His plans were falling into place, and the future was bright indeed. He deserved a reward for his hard work, although he would have found a reason to indulge himself under any circumstances. It was definitely time to celebrate!

The Golden Barb was built on its own pier over the wide harbor that formed this section of the long, serpentine Mekong River. The flamboyant-looking establishment was four stories tall, painted a festive shade of bright yellow, and topped by a high, cobalt-tiled peaked roof in the style of the region. Wide verandas ran around the outside of each level, with sea-green awnings stretching far beyond gold-lacquered deck rails to shade the interior from the Tropic of Cancer's merciless midday sun.

Above the entrance a six-foot-long carving of *The Golden Barb* itself, a kind of giant carp native to the region and a popular symbol of good fortune, hung in front of a painted mural depicting a river bottom. Gold-painted scales twinkled in the late afternoon sunlight, while the breeze from the river caused it to sway slightly, creating the illusion that the eponymous fish was actually alive and swimming lazily along. The species also happened to make a tasty meal, and as attractive as the display was, it only added to Blom's already considerable appetite.

The Golden Barb was a bit on the expensive side, which was just fine with Blom as the prices kept away the riffraff that haunted every harbor. He, while not truly wealthy *(just yet!)* was quite a bit more than comfortably well-off. Despite the high quality and relative safety of *The Golden Barb*, he still wore his scabbarded saber at his side—one could never be too careful. The inn had many fine features to recommend it, but most important of all was the superb cuisine they offered, among the best he had enjoyed on three continents. It had quickly become his eatery of choice in Phnom Penh, and over the last few weeks he had become something of a regular. The owners of the place were said to be a conglomerate of locals, Chinese, and his own Dutch countrymen, and the place attracted people like Blom, bored merchants with substantial amounts of coin burning holes in their pockets.

The doorman, a portly Cambodian gentleman dressed in a black silk suit with coral buttons, ushered Blom in with a deep bow. Blom palmed him a few coins, not too many (after all, he was not rich *just yet!*), but enough that the man always remembered him and gave him the preferred customer treatment. Blom had learned a long time ago that if you are generous with people it would inevitably be repaid tenfold. Blom blinked a few times as his eyes adjusted from the sun's slanted glare to the dim, candlelit interior. The doorman handed him off to the *maître d'*, a serious-faced, thin fellow who stood a head taller than most of the local populace. His uniform was the same cut as the doorman's, but the silk was coral in hue and featured buttons carved from mother of pearl.

"What is your pleasure this evening, Captain Blom?" he asked in accented but quite fluent Dutch. As he made this inquiry, he gave a subtle tilt of his head toward an adjacent parlor, its contents hidden behind a silk curtain. The tinkling laughter of women could be heard emanating from within.

"Tonight I must begin by dining, my good sir. I am positively famished!" Blom told him in his cheerful, booming voice. Then he leaned in closer and added in a softer tone "Perhaps once I have regained my strength I might explore *other* forms of entertainment..." followed by a conspiratorial wink.

The *maître d'* favored him with a broad grin, revealing that the majority of his teeth were a glittering gold, and bowed deeply.

"Whatever you wish, Captain Blom. Please, follow me. Your usual table?"

"Ah, you spoil me. That would be most excellent, kind sir, you run a house without peer."

A waiter dressed in white silk with cerulean blue buttons helped Blom into his seat. The *maître d'* waited for him to scurry off, then spread his hands wide before him.

"It is always a great pleasure to have you here with us, Captain Blom. If you have need of anything, anything at all, by all means, summon me. I am at your service."

"And it is my great pleasure to be here!" Blom meant it from the bottom of his heart. "Thank you so much for your warm welcome, good sir, I always feel at home in *The Golden Barb*."

While he said this he slipped a handful of coins into the *maître d's* open palm, at least three times what the doorman had received. Blom knew which side his bread was buttered on, and felt such a modest investment was worth its weight in gold.

The *maître d'* bowed deeply as he backed away, ending the conversation by assuring him, "the waiters will be here shortly to ask your order, Captain Blom. Enjoy!"

Blom grinned widely. He was a true *bon vivant* as the French said, a man dedicated to the art of good living. With a sigh of relief, he unbuckled his belt under the tablecloth and leaned back into the comfort of the plush velvet cushions of his seat. The evening was off to a wonderful start!

Blom began his meal with a selection of Khmer dishes. One of his favorites was fish *amok*, filets dipped in coconut milk and egg, then seasoned with *kaffir* lime, lemongrass, and other spices. It melted in his mouth, and he enjoyed each bite with relish. He then tucked into some *nom banh chok*, a green fish curry that included shredded banana leaves, beansprouts seasoned with basil, and fresh mint served over rice noodles. It was a very popular local dish that could be found on nearly any street corner, but somehow the chefs at *The Golden Barb* elevated it to a fine art, a steaming bowl of heaven. Having enjoyed enough fish for the time being, it was time for some *lok lak*, stir-fried beef with a variety of succulent fresh vegetables in a rich sauce.

Blom spent the next two hours in a state of bliss, slowly making his way through nearly half of the considerable menu. There was so much to try! He kept careful notes on each dish:when he eventually helped his dear friends the Nishioka family open the restaurant in Grantville he wanted to make sure a wide variety of cuisines from all over Asia were available. Blom truly loved food, and the first thing he had done in that astonishing enclave of time travelers was to eat everything they had. It was mostly excellent, as one might expect from such a fanciful folk. *Cheeseburgers and fries!* One day he would savor such delights again.

Blom could tell that most *American* cuisine had its roots in Europe, but there were some surprises as well, dishes that had sprung from African, Caribbean, Mexican, and indigenous tribal traditions. It was all amazingly delicious, but when he asked Grantvillers what they wanted to eat the most in their new home in space and time, a surprising number named Asian dishes originating from all over the continent! There was sushi, *phad Thai*, *bibimbap*, and something called General Tso's chicken, although the young couple he was talking to had a brief debate over whether that was authentically Chinese in origin.

Blom took it all in, quite literally in the case of his many meals. One fine and pleasant evening while he was relaxing in the famed Thuringen Gardens enjoying some excellent beer, an epiphany came to him—these people (who were richer than Croesus by his accounting) all wanted to eat Asian food, some quite badly, with a yearning that he could well understand, himself being a staunch aficionado of fine international cuisine that was so often difficult to come by. That was when it dawned on him that what the Americans needed was a new restaurant. An Asian restaurant.

It was true that Blom was not the first to think of this. One enterprising person from the *up-time*, who was no more Chinese, or any other kind of Asian, than Blom himself, had opened a restaurant called the Golden Pagoda, claiming to serve Chinese food in an attempt to cash in on the demand. It was mediocre at best. Apparently, they had learned their craft from recipes found in a type of print publication called a *cookbook*. While the food was palatable, it completely lacked the subtleties of the authentic dishes he was accustomed to, and the brown goo that they passed off as *soy sauce* was utterly awful, so much so that he had even overheard other customers complaining about it. Blom allowed himself a small smirk. The art of making proper soy sauce would arrive in Grantville with him and his Nihonmachi contingent, along with a great many other valuable and delicious skills. The restaurant he envisioned would make the poor Golden Pagoda pale in comparison. He might even consider buying them out once they realized their ersatz attempts couldn't possibly compete with the real thing!

It must be destiny, because Blom knew just the people to make his culinary enterprise happen. His dear friend Yoriaki the *bento* boat man was in possession of a living treasure—his lovely wife Momo, who in Blom's estimation was the greatest chef in the world, and she didn't even know it. He had told her as much several times, but she just laughed shyly and replied that he was a flatterer—she was so humble! The *bentos* she created in her modest little kitchen in their modest little house in the city's Japanese conclave had to be experienced to be believed, the perfect marriage of art and culinary science. Momo would be the guiding star of their Grantville establishment, the highly honored head chef, but she wouldn't be alone. He would also recruit from the other wives of Nihonmachi, women from all around the region, many of whom were very fine cooks in their own right.

From that brilliant, shining idea (the Grantvillers portrayed such illuminated thoughts as glowing *light bulbs*, another seeming miracle from their former future), Blom began to piece together a scenario where not only his friends, but maybe even the entire town of Japanese they had helped rescue from the terrible betrayal their turncoat hosts in Ayutthaya perpetrated upon them, could all profit richly from the journey to Europe they were about to embark on. It would be heroic Blom and his kindly uncles who brought them to a new life of opportunity and prosperity they could all share (and own shares) in. He always felt a bit bad about leaving them in Phnom Penh, which was quite a nice town really, but he knew they weren't happy, and now, five years later they still weren't. When he and his uncles made their offer most of them jumped at the chance, eager to take their chances on a new and better life.

And so, they were all going to Grantville, and they would all become filthy rich! Blom smiled at the memory of his uncles witnessing the town from the future for the first time, their eyes goggled out almost as much as the green fish his ship was named after. Despite their astonishment, they quickly ascertained that there were great opportunities to be had, and being quite a bit more than comfortably well off, they began buying up as much property as possible, despite it already being outrageously overpriced in comparison to anywhere else in Europe. They had reasoned that the miraculous event wasn't likely to occur again elsewhere, so they had best act immediately, with full faith that their investments would continue to grow in value. They had been right. Their assets, which were mostly outside of Grantville's original circle, but well within its sphere of immediate influence, and included a highly coveted retail space in Grantville's downtown, had increased exponentially.

Blom emitted a long, loud, satisfied belch. Not wanting to offend, he cupped his hand over his mouth, a bit too late really, while his eyes darted around the room to see if anyone had heard him. The other diners were far enough away that they seemed oblivious, and the staff couldn't care less. The chef would actually be pleased, taking it as a sign that someone appreciated his work. In any case, it served as a signal. It was time to wash that delightful meal down. With a bit of a grunt at the effort (he had, after all, eaten enough for three ordinary men), Blom hoisted himself from his chair and wandered into the bar.

The Golden Barb's lounge was as finely appointed as the rest of the establishment and boasted a crowd despite the early hour. The mood was festive. A group of Dutchmen with whom he was acquainted were raising tankards and laughing loudly beside the long, teak wood bar. They were the most lively bunch in the place, so he headed over to join them.

"*Hallo, vrienden!* May I join you?"

"Blom! *Welkom!*" the cheerful group replied, waving him over and making a space at the bar big enough for him. The captain of an East India Company ship docked just down the quay from *Groenevisch*, Jacop van Noortstrant, clapped him warmly on the arm and said, "You look fresh and well fed this evening, Blom! How goes business?"

"Business goes well, Jacop, very well indeed! In fact, tonight I am celebrating a new venture that seems poised to make us a more than tidy profit. Good times ahead!"

Someone handed him a tankard of a rice-based lager brewed locally in such a way as to appeal to European tastes. He took a long draught of the delicious amber liquid, then raised it in a toast. "*Proost,* my friends, and may such good fortune find us all!"

"We'll all drink to that!" Jacop cried out in a merry tone, and they all did, draining their tankards with gusto. He signaled the barman for another round, then turned back to Blom, not trying to hide his curiosity in the least. "Please, friend Blom, regale us with your tale of success! Tell us all about it!"

And so Blom decided he would—he was fairly bursting to tell someone, anyway! Even so, a note of caution sounded in his mind. These fellows, cordial though they may be, were still his competitors in some ways, and he would need to keep a few important details to himself while giving them the gist of it.

"Well, on my latest trip back to Europe, my uncles and I paid a visit to *Grantville...*" Once he uttered that magic word the group quieted down and began to listen. Even the barman and his assistant, who were in the practice of studiously ignoring any customer conversation unless it was a request for service, leaned subtly toward them from across the bar to over-hear the tale. Although they were locals, they had undoubtedly acquired some Dutch through the course of their employment, and Blom held their rapt attention.

Everyone in the world was curious about Grantville, yet so far only a few had actually set foot in the place. Now here was Blom, who had spent several weeks there, and his accounts of the wonders of the future were thrilling to hear. He began with the mechanical monsters called "automo-biles" driving around without horses, lights in the street without burning flames, people speaking to each other while miles apart, and much more. Eventually he came to his business plans.

"The people from the future love food. They have made something of a hobby out of it, sharing recipes and holding cooking competitions. Even the children have developed the tastes of a gastronomist! So, this is something I hold in common with them!"

Everyone laughed at that, as Blom's ravenous appetite was well known around the docks.

"In the future they came from, cuisines from all around the world were readily available, even in what they describe as 'sleepy little Grantville'! Nearly everyone I talked to mentioned a desire for food from the East. As you probably know, I am a connoisseur of Oriental cuisines myself, and it just so happens that among my all-time favorites are the Japanese *bento* lunches my good friend Yoriaki sells along the docks here, just as he did back in Ayutthaya. And now, he will be traveling with me to Grantville to ply his trade there, albeit in a proper eatery much like *The Golden Barb* here instead of from a little boat, to what I am sure will be a very enthusiastic clientele!"

A murmur went through the crowd; Blom was not the *bento* man's only fan. Nearly all gathered had tried the *bentos* and agreed they tasted heavenly. Blom drained his tankard during the pause. He was feeling very, very fine, sharing his good fortune with like-minded comrades such as these gave him great satisfaction. Jacop signaled the barkeep for another round, then continued the conversation.

"Yes, that fellow is a wonderful cook. Everyone agrees he has real talent."

Blom laughed. "Ah, a common misconception. My dear friend Yoriaki *sells* the *bentos*, but the mastermind behind it all is actually his charming wife, Momo, who *makes* them!"

Blom was too caught up in his story to notice the exchange of glances that took place between the barkeep and his assistant, or the fact that the assistant took his leave soon after, slipping silently out the back into the sultry Phnom Penh night.

* * *

Late the next morning Blom awoke from a troubled sleep, his sheets soaked in sweat. The excesses of the night before had little effect on him. He was too experienced a merrymaker to suffer much of a hangover. Even so, he felt off, and he groaned as he lifted his considerable bulk out of bed. After splashing some water on his face, he gazed into the small mirror he kept on his dresser just in time to see a look of horror pass across his usually jovial face.

"Oh, dear God. I think I've done something bad..." he murmured to himself. His mind went back to the events of the night before, going over everything he had said to the gathering. Soon enough he arrived at the utterance that had come back to haunt him.

"Momo," he whispered. "I said her name." Now that he was no longer under the influence of a jolly mood and a large number of tankards of beer, he recalled what Yoriaki had told him about life in Phnom Penh.

"I keep a low profile here, Blom. The Mekong is much more dangerous than the Chao Phraya ever was. There are several gangs of thugs, river pirates that would like nothing better than to skin me alive since I refuse to pay their tolls. I go home a different way every night and never tell anyone about my family."

Blom slapped his forehead in shame.

"Idiot! You told *everyone there* her name!" He knew all too well how gossip traveled fast along the docks. There was a good chance that every scoundrel who had ever crossed Yoriaki's path was now tracking down his wife's whereabouts, with all roads leading to Nihonmachi.

Moving faster than one might think a bulky fellow like Blom could, he slipped on his clothes and boots, then the belt that carried his cutlass and hand ax, followed by the blunderbuss that rode over his shoulder on a leather strap—all the gear he would use in the event that his ship was ever boarded by pirates. He then paid a visit to his dresser, opened the bottom drawer, then felt around in its furthermost recesses until his fingers fell on a rectangular wooden case, which he carefully extricated—it was quite heavy.

"Ah yes, my pretty souvenir from Grantville. I can only pray your services will not be required." he said to himself, but his gut told him otherwise.

Nihonmachi, Phnom Penh, Kingdom of Khmer, Indochina
1635

Nishioka Momo knew she was in trouble. She could hear heavy footsteps coming across the hard clay yard from the marsh's edge toward the house, then up the steps that led to the wide porch surrounding the main floor, which was perched on three-yard-high stilts in case of flooding. All the doors and windows were locked, a matter of policy although they would offer scant protection from a determined intruder. She stood frozen, silent, gripping the hilt of the *wakizashi* blade her husband had gifted her for comfort as she waited to see what would come next.

A loud rap at the door broke the silence, then another. Could it be her husband returning early, along with guests? That small hope was dashed as a rough male voice called out in Khmer, the Cambodian language.

"*Momo*, are you home? Come out, we wish to buy your *bento* lunches! We are so hungry!" This was followed by coarse laughter from other men. She guessed there were at least four of them, maybe more.

"I will make some *special bento* for *you*," she hissed under her breath.

"Momo, it's so rude of you not to welcome your guests! Come out now, or I assure you, we *will* come in!"

The door, which was sturdy wood, began to rattle. Movement caught her eyes: through the opaque white rice paper windows a dim figure could be seen creeping along the porch. Those windows were *not* sturdy, and could be broken through with little trouble. The shadow paused, then began to bang on the paper. It was strong enough to resist that, but now the long, narrow form of a *dav* sword could be seen, poised to cut through.

Momo made her move. She sprinted across the firm but springy tatami rice mat floor to the window, her *wakizashi* held high at the ready. The intruder's blade poked through a square near the edge with an awful tearing sound, then an arm entered the hole and began to feel about, searching for a latch. Momo brought her blade down hard on the man's wrist in a swift slicing motion. The severed hand fell to the floor, still twitching as blood spurted from the stump, showering the flaxen floor with steaming red spray. The man's screams brought his companions to his side, and there was a moment of cursing confusion as they pushed him out of their way.

A sword blade thrust through the window in a blind attempt to stab whoever was inside. She had been ready for that, and when the hand on the hilt entered, she cut it off, too, sending hand and blade clattering to the floor. That was two out of the fight, at least for the moment. Howls of rage from outside ensued, which bought her scant seconds to decide what to do next. She had been lucky pulling her trick twice. Stupid as they were, they knew better now. Just as she was moving away toward the back of the house, a man's body came crashing through the window, splintering the wooden frame. They had used one of the men she had just injured as a battering ram. He fell to the floor in a heap, moaning as he clutched his bleeding stump. Momo wasted no time. She sprinted into the brick room that housed their commode and laundry, closed and locked the door behind her.

The cool darkness soothed her for a moment. It was time to leave. She pushed a large wash tub across the flagstone floor to reveal a hidden hatchway, which she pulled open. Its well-oiled hinges made no sound. This was their emergency exit, with a sturdy wooden work table placed beneath it. Shoving her blade into the *obi* sash around her waist, she lowered herself down to the tabletop, then pulled the tub back across the opening. They would follow eventually, but she had bought herself some time. She cast her eyes around the dimly lit space under the house, partially hidden from view behind a wall of beans and flowering vines, the warm scent of wisteria a comfort against the cold fear making the blood pound against her eardrums.

"Calm. I must stay calm. The Lord will protect me," she told herself in a quiet voice as she caught her breath.

Above her, she could hear the bandits rummaging around the house in search of her and any spoils they might find. She heard the sound of shattering pottery and froze—*Kannon-Sama!* Her heart sank at the thought of the pretty little statue lying in shards on the floor, one of the few mementos of her mother and Japan she had left. Strangely, despite the sense of loss, the sound of its destruction caused Momo's fear to fade, replaced by a seething rage.

"These men will pay for this intrusion," she vowed.

But first, she needed a plan.

* * *

Nishioka Yoriaki paddled his boat at a feverish pace through the twisting waterways, the veins of the great marsh that crowded the banks of the Mekong River for miles along its course. He knew his way well and took the most direct route possible, his arms a blur as he pumped the paddle into the dark stagnant water. His wife was in danger, and he must come to her aid as soon as he humanly could, if not sooner. He was nearing the turn to the narrow tributary that bordered his home when a boat surged out of a byway ahead, blocking his progress.

"*Kuso*," he cursed under his breath. "Shit! Not again!"

"Hey, Yoriaki!" A corpulent, swarthy fellow dressed in faded silk robes called out to him from the deck of the boat, which was nearly three times the size of his. He was undoubtedly the leader, his tone mocking and his cruel face a study in smug overconfidence.

"We heard you were leaving town and we have come to settle your debt to us!" The man laughed loudly, a snorting guffaw joined by a chorus of eight more men of his ilk, yet another of the river's many gangs of bandits.

Although he knew it was in vain, Yoriaki called back. "I don't have time for this. Please get out of my way."

That only had the effect of making the group laugh even louder. Enough was enough. This time Yoriaki didn't participate in any further banter, even as the leader continued to taunt him. He simply continued to paddle until his bow nudged the side of the enemy's craft. The bandits looked a bit nonplussed, but with a collective shrug they began to jump down into his boat, their *dav* swords at the ready. Without saying a word, Yoriaki reached down to the hidden compartment beside him.

Click.

* * *

The clatter of the men invading her home filled Momo with wrath, but she knew that she must be clever to prevail. She glanced over to the road just a few yards away, but it was still too far to run to safety. Their house was a long way down from the next, and the men would surely catch her if she tried. She heard a loud bang, the front door being shoved open, and saw a pair of legs coming down the steps. She wanted to cut them out from under him, but she couldn't get there in time. She needed to hide, and quickly.

She crouched behind a large clay urn that collected rainwater from a pipe running down from the roof, wondering where to go next. Then it dawned on her. "*Baka*! You fool! Get in *there!*" she whispered under her breath. The urn was a full two meters in circumference, and nearly three meters tall. She carefully pushed its wooden lid halfway open, and, using an overturned bucket as a step, she climbed up and into it, sliding headfirst into the cool, musty water. She was careful not to cut herself with her blade as she performed an underwater flip and came to the surface. The urn was—thankfully—not completely full, so she had a foot of air between her and the lid, which she carefully slid back in place until just a sliver of light remained. Would they find her here? It was a temporary refuge at best. They were ignorant scoundrels, to be sure, but also crafty in the way of wild predators. If only Yoriaki would come home! She prayed for his speedy rescue, keeping the *wakizashi* held at the ready to thrust it upward at any foe unfortunate enough to come looking.

* * *

Old Sokha the noodle vendor pushed his ramshackle cart down the dusty streets of Nihonmachi, leaving a delicious-smelling cloud of charcoal smoke and steaming soup drifting behind him as he went. *If they smell that, they have no choice but to buy*! he thought to himself with a smile. It was after lunch, so he left the settlement's center to visit the more out-of-the-way corners in the hope of scaring up a few more noodle eaters. His noodle soup appealed to all the inhabitants of the enclave, Japanese and otherwise, so he maintained a thriving business. Sokha was a friendly old fellow, generous with his portions, and well loved by all, a welcome fixture in the community. Today he would pay a visit to his good friend Momo out by the swamp's edge: she relished his cooking as much as he loved hers, always resulting in a mutually delicious trade.

The street was quiet as usual, a few scattered homes peeking out from behind woven bamboo fences, their occupants mostly gone off to work for the day. He rounded a gentle curve lined by an unkempt hedge of wild brush of the kind that thrived beside the swamp's damp shores. Momo's place was just ahead, but something made him stop. He heard men talking loudly in Khmer, something of an oddity for the time and place. Perhaps the Nishioka family had hired some workmen for something? They were far enough off that he couldn't make out exactly what they were saying, but as he came closer he could discern that the tone seemed rough, like the barking of unfriendly street dogs.

"That's strange," he mumbled under his breath. He cocked his head to listen more carefully, but his hearing was no longer what it once was, so he set the brake on his cart and began to walk closer, instinctively keeping near the wall of brush and moving slowly so as not to draw attention to himself. He was still some thirty yards away when three thuggish-looking fellows burst out from the front door, all carrying *dav* swords. Sokha stopped dead in his tracks, staring in abject horror at the sight.

"Oh, poor Momo! Surely she is in trouble, and I'll wager Yoriaki has not yet returned from his rounds!"

His hand dropped to his belt, but the sword that had once hung there in his youth had long since been replaced by a soup ladle. With a chagrined frown, he carefully stepped backwards into the hedge's shade. The scoundrels, even if they did happen to see him there, paid him no notice; they were too intent on whatever business was at hand, and whatever that was must surely be foul. Sokha took a few more steps backwards until he was sure he had gone unnoticed, turned, and ran as fast as he could back to the town's center, leaving his cart to steam alone by the side of the road.

* * *

Yoriaki wiped the blood from his *katana* on the robes of the now deceased gang leader who continued to stare up at him from the bottom of the boat despite the fact that his throat had been cut from ear to ear. His face had such a look of surprise on it that Yoriaki shrugged his shoulders and said, "I told you I didn't have time for this and to get out of the way!" before he dragged the dead man up out of the blood-soaked fore and dumped him over the side to join the rest of his crew in their watery grave.

Scowling mightily at the rude interruption and the time it had cost him, Yoriaki managed to shove the now ownerless pirate boat back into the opening in the wall of marsh grass it had come out of just far enough that he could maneuver his much smaller craft around it, and continue on his way. Before he resumed his frantic paddling, he placed his *katana* on the seat in front of him with almost tender care. A truer friend and ally would be hard to find. There was no point in putting the crimson-stained blade back in its hiding place now. He had little doubt it would taste blood again on this darkest of days.

* * *

Momo shivered in the chill water of the urn as it slowly sapped the warmth from her lithe form. Her hands, now white and wrinkled, gripped the hilt of her *wakizashi* tightly despite the numbness creeping into them. She had been in her wet refuge for at least half an hour now, all the while listening intently to the conversation of the invaders just outside. They were frustrated that they hadn't found her yet, but knew that she couldn't get far without them spotting her, so they continued to search the grounds, dumping out large boxes and emptying closets in hope of catching their elusive prey.

She whispered a fervent prayer under her breath. "O merciful Mother Mary, I beg you to protect me now in my hour of utmost need. Please send my beloved husband home in time to save me from these terrible men, I beseech you!" She released one hand from her sword's hilt just long enough to cross herself under the dark water.

"She has got to be here somewhere, dammit!" The voice was uncomfortably close by.

"More boats have arrived with more of our men to help us look," another of the scoundrels announced.

"Is the boss with them?"

"No, not yet. He took a group out toward the river to find the samurai."

Momo's heart sank. "Yoriaki!" she whispered, fighting back tears. She took a shaky breath and blew it out slowly. It was critical that she remain calm, taking a moment to remind herself that her husband was a mighty warrior more than capable of handling a bunch of ragtag thugs like these on his own!

"He has trails cut into the marsh all over the place around here," one of the men said. "Maybe she slipped into one of those? Let's search there next."

Momo didn't quite dare to let out a sigh of relief, holding it in until she thought she heard the men exiting from under the house. She was shaking with cold now. Despite the country's infernal heat, the water was frigid, and she had been in it too long. She was going to have to get out soon, rescued or not. While she considered her next move, with no good options present, her hand was forced. There was still a bandit nearby. She could hear him mumbling irritably to himself. There was a pause, then she clearly heard him say a bit louder, "Well, well, what have we here?" A shadow fell across the sliver of light between the wooden lid and the urn's ceramic edge. Hands appeared, pushing the lid back to make the opening wider, then a face peered in over the edge. "I wonder if there are any fish swimming in here? Perhaps the one that got away?"

"No, it's just the bait," she hissed as she performed the move she had been waiting for, practicing in her head as she counted the long minutes in her dark, wet refuge. Her blade shot up from beneath the surface, its sharp point driving deep into the intruder's right eye. Much to her relief he didn't have time to scream. The *wakizashi* killed him instantly with just the one thrust. She pulled the sword back out with a sickening sucking noise. Several drops of blood fell into the water with tinkling little splashes just before the dead man slid out of view down the side of the urn, into a limp heap on the ground.

She remained there for a long moment, breathing hard, shaking from the cold and the sheer terror of what had just transpired.

"Get out, Momo! You have to *get out!*" she told herself. Her muscles ached after holding still for so long in the cold. Eventually someone would discover her victim, and more heads would appear. If she didn't make her move now she would be trapped, playing the part of the fish in the barrel, which never ended well for the fish. She slowly pushed the lid off, taking a moment to scan the surroundings. No one was under the house currently, so, with a silent apology to her *wakizashi*, she let it drop safely to the ground before she crawled out, being careful not to step on the dead man who lay sprawled beneath her. The gruesome sight made her chill all the more uncomfortable. Momo then took a moment to crouch beside her uncomfortable sanctuary, rubbing her limbs to restore circulation while resisting a rising sense of panic.

What could she do? Where could she go? Her enemy had increased in number. At least five of them cast about in the front yard, and who knew how many more out back, or in the house above? Oh, if only her dear Yoriaki would come! "Please Dear God, let him be safe! Bring him to me soon, I don't know how much longer I can last!" Her whispered prayer bolstered her courage. Momo's faith was strong. It had seen her family through great danger before, surely the Lord Jesus loved her, and would see to it that they prevailed again.

There was a cluster of bandits near the wooden front steps, which provided a slight amount of cover. Where could she go? Through the bean vines that were trellised along the house's side, she could see that a sentry had been posted along the road. There was no way she could make it past him without being found out. Running barefoot down the hot, gravelly track would surely end in disaster. They would most certainly catch her long before she could even reach the closest neighbor, and, even if she did, what could poor old Grandmother Sano do but die with her at the hands of these murderous curs?

No, escape was not an option. She must remain here and stay hidden until help arrived. She looked down at the dead eyes of the man she had just killed. His sightless stare was unnerving. She needed to move.

The only cover available was the brick-walled laundry room under the commode. Keeping low and moving as silently as possible, she scuttled across the hard earthen floor. Hiding just inside the doorless opening, she caught her breath, forcing herself to stay calm.

She had barely managed to catch her breath when a cry went up outside. "Where is Nhean?"

"He went under the house a little while ago. He should have been back by now."

"Well, let's go find him!"

So, the man she had killed had a name. *Nhean.* Yes, he had been a terrible man who would have most certainly killed her, but he was still a person, and now he was dead by her hand. He wasn't the first man she had killed with the *wakizashi* her husband had gifted her in Ayutthaya, in what now seemed like a dream life. It had been necessary to make her escape from that blood-soaked river shore. Now, once again, her life depended on her skill with the blade, and she could only hope the good Lord would forgive her the blood she spilled. Her hand instinctively tightened on its handle as she prayed again for Yoriaki to return before she must put it to work again.

Unfortunately, that was not to be. Five men entered the shadowy realm under the house, their dark eyes burning with hatred and frustration.

It wouldn't take them long to find Nhean's corpse. When they did, they would sound the alarm, which would draw a hornet's nest full of angry men down upon her. Now there were only five of them. Momo made her decision then, possibly the most difficult she would ever face. She stepped out of the laundry room, holding her blade behind her, out of sight.

"Looking for me?" she called out in her slightly accented Khmer, wearing a wan smile.

The quizzical look on the bandits' dirty faces was almost worth it. The last thing they had expected was for her to show herself willingly. Wide, rapacious grins appeared as they made their way toward her. She hoped they wouldn't notice dead Nhean as they passed by the urn. She wanted them to think she was helpless, although she had already parted two of them from their sword hands, she thought with a grim satisfaction. Still, they hadn't actually seen her do it, so they might think there was someone else in the house helping her, which, unfortunately, there was not. Her hopes were rewarded. All their attention was on her now.

One of the bandits smiled and gave her a small bow, a cruel mockery of politeness.

"Well, it looks like we have found our little mouse! There are no more holes to run to now!" he mocked her in a childlike tone that made the others laugh.

Momo simmered with hatred, the handle of her *wakizashi* hidden behind her back a comforting weight. *We shall see who is the cat and who are the mice.* She felt a bit surprised that the fear she should be feeling had subsided, replaced with a cold rage, but forced herself to appear to be frightened.

"You're not going to hurt me, are you?" she asked in what she hoped was a suitably pathetic tone.

All the bandits laughed as they continued their approach. The one who had spoken replied, "Oh no, pretty little Momo mouse, we are just here to *play* with you!"

Momo's heart beat fast, but she took deep, calming breaths, noting that the bandits were off their guard, considering her to be easy prey. A feeling of steely resolve filled her, erasing any remaining fear. *So they want to play? They will find that this mouse has claws.*

The talkative fellow was the first to step in close. He reached for her with both grimy hands after shoving his blade into his belt, which would prove to be a fatal error. Momo brought the *wakizashi* out from behind her back to shove it into his belly in one swift motion. The look of surprise in his bulging eyes might have been comical in other circumstances, his rapacious expression now a death grin.

Before the others had any idea that she had killed the first of them, she had pushed the dying bandit into the scoundrel coming in beside him from the left to join in the fun. He instinctively caught the corpse of his comrade as it slumped toward him, making it impossible for him to take a swing with his sword. Momo used the opportunity to slice his throat open. Her former-samurai husband made sure the family blades stayed sharp and had made her practice her swing until it was nearly as natural as breathing. Seeing how easily she had dispatched two of her assailants, Momo laughed, a strange, wild sound that almost frightened her more than the danger before her. This was much easier than splitting open the coconuts she had trained on!

The remaining three bandits were staring in disbelief at what had just happened: the mouse they expected was actually a cat in disguise, and her claws were sharp and swift. Momo could tell that her eerie laugh had shaken them up even more, so she did it again as she drove the *wakizashi* into the next-in-line's gut, causing him to drop his blade and double over, his hands trying to stop the gushing blood that stained his ragged trousers red.

Three down, two to go.

The two remaining snapped out of their stupors and raised their *dav* swords to defend themselves. Their blades were larger and heavier than hers, so Momo would be at a disadvantage if it came to parrying. She had seen cats fight and knew that her only hope was to emulate their relentless assaults. Momo was smaller and faster than they were, an advantage. She jumped to the side of the closest bandit, avoiding his larger blade's rather slow swing, which swiped through the empty air where she had been a moment ago, and ran the *wakizashi* across his exposed throat. Some part of her subconscious bemoaned the mess she was making under her house, which made her laugh again.

Unfortunately, the fifth bandit had finally awakened to the danger he faced and was backing away from the carnage, his *dav* held in front of him in a defensive posture, making him a much greater challenge than his foolish friends had been. Coming to his senses, he cried out for reinforcements, "She's here, and she's armed! Come quick, and beware!"

Momo's heart sank. She knew she had been extremely lucky so far, wringing the element of surprise for every drop of advantage it had held. That cloth was dry now. Her enemies would be well aware of the danger she posed, and would come in greater numbers to overwhelm her. Even so, she would not go down easily.

With a feral snarl that again surprised the part of her mind that was standing aside watching in disbelief at her newfound ferociousness, Momo ran at the last bandit. He was ready for her, and, while no samurai, he managed a surprisingly agile sidestep while his blade landed a long, deep cut on her forearm. Momo noted the rather alarming amount of blood seeping out of the fresh wound, but was so full of adrenaline she barely felt it.

The bandit's courage returned along with his overconfidence. He allowed himself a victorious laugh at his successful strike, which gave Momo the moment she needed to come in close enough to drive her now-crimson-stained blade between his ribs and into his lung. The look of surprise on his face as he fell to his knees pleased her in a way she never would have considered, and she began to fear what her God, who had told her plainly *Thou shalt not kill* in the Holy Scriptures, would think of his murderous lamb now.

Momo would have to confess her sins later. Her latest casualty's summons for aid was answered as four more bandits made their way under the house from the yard. There was little doubt more would come now that they had found her. Still several yards away, they blinked in the gloom for a moment as their eyes adjusted, then beheld the carnage she had wrought, with stunned expressions that quickly shifted to wrath.

"You little bitch! We're going to make you pay for this!" the closest of them shouted at her as they raised their *davs* to begin their attack.

Somehow, Momo remained calm despite knowing her end might be near. She would not go down easily and intended to make her husband proud. Yoriaki had trained her well, but against these odds...

* * *

Old Sokha ran back into the main part of Nihonmachi as fast as his sandaled feet could carry him, gasping a bit, but in reasonably good condition for a man of fifty-nine years, thanks to the daily exercise of pushing his noodle cart around. As he neared the central plaza he began to shout out in his rudimentary Japanese, "*Abunai!* Danger!" There were only a few people about, but they all stopped what they were doing to see what the commotion was about.

Sokha came to a stop in front of the large imposing home of Ishida, a rich merchant and one of the community's leaders. Ishida's Cambodian majordomo appeared in the door, a questioning look on his face. Sokha caught his breath, then implored him in Khmer. "Please, tell Master Ishida that Nihonmachi is under attack by river pirates! They are at the Nishioka house, and poor Momo is probably home alone! Please, you must send help!"

By then a small crowd had gathered, mostly women out doing their shopping and a few of the town's craftsmen, all with looks of concern on their faces.

The majordomo nodded his understanding and disappeared into the gloom beyond the tiled *genkan* entryway, where shoes were deposited before entering the house proper through a curtain. Not more than thirty seconds later, Ishida himself appeared, dressed in simple *yukata* summer robes, and carrying his samurai swords in their ornate scabbards. Ishida was one of Sokha's best customers, and the noodle vendor was sure he would take his warning seriously.

"Noodle man! These river pirates are at the Nishioka home, you say?" he asked Sokha in relatively clear Khmer.

"Yes, Master Ishida!" Foreseeing Ishida's next question, he quickly added, "There are at least three of them, but I think there were more in the house! Please, you must go help them. Oh, poor Momo!" Sokha was very fond of the Nishiokas, especially Momo with whom he shared a bond based on their love of cooking. He had never told anyone else his secret soup recipe, but he had given it to Momo, after extracting an oath of silence from her that was to last until his death.

"Of course!" Ishida replied, with a brief nod of appreciation for the warning. He then switched to Japanese to announce in booming tones, "Our friends the Nishioka family are under attack from river pirates! Anyone who can fight, go grab a weapon and join me. We will teach these riffraff scum a hard lesson for troubling our brother and sister! Now, hurry and come along with me!"

At Ishida's command the gathered crowd, which had quickly grown in numbers, murmured their agreement and scattered, running back to their homes to gather whatever arms they could muster. Unfortunately, most of the town's active samurai were elsewhere around Phnom Penh, employed as guards and hired swords for the city's wealthy and powerful. Still, many of the craftsmen had been samurai once, and they soon returned bearing their warrior weapons, although some of them looked a bit dusty. Those with no martial training brought kitchen cleavers, axes, picks, and hoes, whatever they could manage to scrounge together. Within a few minutes, Ishida strode along the dusty road toward the Nishioka home with Sokha at his side, followed by around twenty armed villagers.

Sokha was pleased that he had been able to summon help, but his heart was filled with fear for his friend as he led the hastily assembled force toward awaiting peril.

* * *

Yoriaki turned his small boat into the rush-lined canal that led to his home. He rounded the final bend to find his way blocked by a row of six larger boats. The walls of vegetation were so close that there was no room to paddle past them. Muttering a string of curses in all the languages he knew, which made for a considerable collection of profanities and vulgarities, he pulled up behind the last in line, tightened his sword belt, and climbed up onto the aft deck. This afforded him a view forward. Most of the parked boats were empty, but there were a few bandits still making their way across the planks toward the small dock he had constructed on his back garden's patch of beach. Beyond that, the house was still obscured by the tall reeds and marsh grasses.

Yoriaki, an able boatman, swiftly ran along the thirty-odd feet of rough decking to the prow, then leaped from there onto the aft of the next in line, continuing to do so until he arrived at the second boat out from his dock.

There he caught up to three bandits doing the same, latecomers to the grim gathering that was taking place at his home. Apparently, every scum and villain on the Mekong had decided to attend. Yoriaki might have felt a bit proud at having irritated so many hooligans if the circumstances were less desperate.

Yoriaki silently drew his blade as he came up behind them. He rather casually relieved the first of his head, then the next. The third heard the thumping noise of severed heads bouncing off the deck planks and turned to be rewarded with a fatal slash to his throat.

Yoriaki leaped off the last boat onto his dock running, entering his garden to find a group of ten more river pirates making their way toward his house. He couldn't see past them, but heard the sound of clashing blades coming from the open space beneath the dwelling, and his heart filled with a desperate hope—could it be his dear Momo making a stand with the *wakizashi* he had insisted she learn to defend herself with? Barely slowing down, Yoriaki penetrated the group from behind, his blade moving at a blur, slashing and cutting his way through the crowd as if they were just an inconvenient growth of shrubbery obstructing the garden path. The river pirates toppled over right and left into puddles formed from their own gushing blood. They had thought to bring trouble to his home, to his family, and now they would pay for that transgression with their lives.

Momo stood her ground, dodging the rather clumsy blows of her assailants, using her small stature and swiftness to every advantage. She had killed three more, but six more had just joined them, and she began to accept that her end was drawing near. The deep slash she had suffered to her arm was still running red, her ceaseless movements never giving her a chance to stem the flow. She was tired now, and she would eventually succumb to the blood loss if her attackers didn't kill her first.

There was a brief lull in the combat. Momo crouched like the cat she imagined she had become, ready to swipe her deadly claw at whoever came at her next. That is when several things happened.

First, she heard a commotion from the road, what sounded like an approaching crowd in the middle distance, joined by the pounding of a horse's hooves approaching their gate.

Next, she heard the sound of swordplay coming from the back garden. She saw a man completely covered with blood slashing his way through a group of approaching bandits. It took her a moment to realize who it was—Yoriaki! She called to him as loudly as she could, but her voice came out strangled and hoarse from exhaustion. "Yoriaki! I am here!"

It was loud enough, and Yoriaki heard it over the curses of the dying and those who would be joining them in short order. "Momo! I am coming!"

Much to Yoriaki's chagrin the bandits had managed to form a line, and were now putting up a resistance, blocking his path to his beleaguered wife. He redoubled his attacks, fighting with a fury that would have made the ancient gods of war take pause before engaging him.

At the same moment, fresh assailants reached Momo and began to swing at her. She dodged the first, but the next came in low, landing a painful blow on her outer thigh, causing her to lose her balance and fall.

Yoriaki saw this and screamed with frustration. "MOMO!" Would the good Lord be so cruel as to bring him this close to saving the love of his life, only to make him watch as these animals cut her down? Tears ran from his eyes as he fought with every ounce of his power and prowess.

The scoundrel who had managed to cut his wife and take her down now stood over her, uttering a gloating laugh that filled Yoriaki's vision with a field of red sparks. The bandit raised his *dav* to strike her again as Yoriaki struggled to reach her.

Momo fell badly, landing on her side. The pain of her leg wound nearly made her pass out. Despite this she still held her *wakizashi* in an unbreakable grip and raised it to counter the blow she saw coming, knowing it wouldn't be fast enough to stop the *dav's* heavy, curved blade from cleaving her skull.

The fervent prayer she was whispering, undoubtedly her last, was cut short by a loud CRACK from the front garden. A round hole appeared in the forehead of her would-be murderer. His eyes rolled back in his head as blood began to seep from it. He fell in a heap beside her.

The CRACK sounded again, and another approaching bandit came to a sudden halt, a bloodstain forming around a fresh hole in his shirt over his belly. He fell to the ground next to his recently deceased comrade.

A third CRACK resounded, but the remaining bandits remained standing. All stared in stunned surprise in the direction of the sounds, not sure whether to engage the source or run away.

This was shortly followed by a loud curse in Dutch, the male voice familiar...

Three more CRACKS came in rapid succession, resulting in three more holes in her assailants: one through an eye, one through the heart, and the last another gut shot. All three men collapsed like marionettes with their strings cut.

Momo managed to turn toward the source of the loud noises. Their dear friend Blom stood a few yards away holding some kind of a pistol in front of him that looked like a child's toy, far too small to have done the kind of fatal damage she had witnessed. She summoned a smile for him, then everything went dark.

* * *

Keep watch for the third story in this sequence.

The State Library Papers
Non-fiction

Flint's Shards, Inc.

Something Old, Something New: A Materials of Construction Survey

Iver P. Cooper

What we can construct—whether it be a building, a boiler, or a toaster—and how well it performs its function depends on the materials incorporated into it. One of the effects of the Ring of Fire will be an ever-expanding palette of materials of construction for the engineer. Depending on their properties and cost, they may be used as structural materials or as protective coverings for another material.

Since I wrote "Mineral Mastery" (*Grantville Gazette* 23), "Industrial Alchemy, Part 2: Inorganic Chemical Bestiary" (*Grantville Gazette* 26), and "Industrial Alchemy Part 5: Polymers" (*Grantville Gazette* 29), the timeline of the 1632 universe has advanced from 1634 to 1637, and there is a need to provide an updated materials survey to reflect additional canon. In addition, unlike those prior articles, this one focuses on construction materials.

I have divided this article into three sections. First, the materials available to down-timers prior to the Ring of Fire. For these materials, I have tried to provide price information, even though it is difficult to assess how the prices will change in the new timeline (NTL). Note that Gorg Huff estimated an exchange rate of 42 guilders per New United States dollar, corresponding in purchase power (with caveats) to the 2000 US dollar. And to put that in perspective, an outdoor laborer might earn 6.5 guilders per week and a master carpenter 9 (Van Osnabrugge).

Second, up-time materials that have already been canonized. (This is of course a moving target; this article can't cover materials first canonized after it is published—unless I get my own time machine.) This article will point out what is said in canon about them.

Finally, up-time materials that have yet to be canonized. I will talk about how they are made and how soon I think they will be available.

One important property of materials of construction that I am going to skirt here is corrosion resistance, and that's because it deserves a separate article. However, I will acknowledge here what up-time literature says about how a material was used in the "future past."

Down-Time Materials of Construction

Tin

Tin is obtained from cassiterite (tin oxide) by carbothermal reduction. It is a soft metal, used both directly (as tin plate) and in alloys with copper. In 1631, English tin sold for about six guilders per 100 pounds (Posthumus). Its use in cold climates is limited by its susceptibility to transformation to powdery gray tin. Inorganic tin compounds are non-toxic but organic ones are poisonous. In the modern world, it has retained its old uses (in pewter and bell metal) and acquired new ones (in solder, Babbitt metal, and dental amalgams). Tin is also used in the Pilkington float glass process (1952).

Lead

While used by down-timers for pipes, bullets, printing type, roofing material, and, alloyed with tin, in pewter tableware, lead metal will acquire new uses subsequent to the Ring of Fire. Its use in lead-acid batteries has been canonized, and it is likely that it is also used as a solder in the electrical industry.

Lead, unfortunately, is neither strong nor hard, and its high density is a disadvantage for many applications. Moreover, while it was used for plumbing by the Romans, corrosion of the pipes would contaminate the drinking water with poisonous lead compounds.

The leading lead ore is galena (lead sulfide), but cerussite (lead carbonate), anglesite (lead sulfate), pyromorphite (lead chloride phosphate) and boulangerite (lead antimony sulfide) have also been mined. Galena is roasted in air, yielding the oxide, which is then subjected to carbothermal reduction. There are methods for recovering the associated copper, silver, and gold, but they may be left in deliberately to increase corrosion resistance.

In April 1631, English lead sold for 6.68 guilders per hundred pounds. The price climbed steadily after that, to 8.40 in May 1636 OTL and then dropped to 7.35 in June 1638 OTL (Posthumus).

Chemical lead is "lead refined to a copper content of 0.04 to 0.08 percent and a silver content of 0.002 to 0.02 percent." Terne metal is a lead alloy with 10-15% tin (EB15).

Zinc

The Europeans already use calamine (a zinc carbonate, with some zinc silicate) to make brass, a copper-zinc alloy. Elemental zinc was first made in India and then China. In Europe, Paracelsus is believed to have made zinc, and alchemists may have used it to make zinc oxide. Zinc was also an occasional byproduct of lead smelters. However, Europe was still importing zinc from India and China even in the eighteenth century.

The metal is used in modern times to galvanize steel, as a sacrificial anode, and as the anode in several battery chemistries. While it is not usually considered a structural metal, rolled zinc sheeting was used in nineteenth-century Paris as a roofing material (Emsley 657).

In the period immediately after the Ring of Fire, zinc is earmarked for military use (brass cartridges, I presume) and in Grantville, zinc pennies and zinc stripped off unusable galvanized steel are recycled ("Recycling," Schillawski and Rigby, *Grantville Gazette* 6). A USE embassy arrives in Venice in February 1634 and in April, Magda and Sharon order two hundred tons of "Japanese" [sic, Chinese] zinc for delivery to Grantville by midsummer 1635 (*1634: The Galileo Affair*, Flint and Dennis, Chapter 29).

By February 1634, a Jena academic alchemist has written an article on how to isolate zinc from calamine and the way the article read suggested that the process had been carried out, at least on a laboratory scale. Also by that date, Dr. Gribbleflotz had isolated four thousand *pfund* (pounds) of pure zinc metal from sphalerite (zincblende; zinc sulfide), found in the Harz Mountains ("Dr. Phil Zinkens a Bundle," *1636: The Chronicles of Dr. Gribbleflotz*, Offord and Boatright, Chapter 14).

The first historical European (Amsterdam) price I have for zinc is 25 guilders for 100 pounds "spelter" in 1722 (Posthumus). "Spelter" is a problematic term that can refer to zinc, a zinc-lead alloy, or a zinc-copper alloy.

In 1737, zinc (probably a crude zinc called tutenague) sold for 6.6 taels per picul in Canton and 8.1 in Amoy (Tagliacozzo 133). A picul was what a man could carry on a shoulder pole and in 1844 Hong Kong it was defined as 133.33 pounds (Wikipedia). A tael was about 40 grams silver (purity uncertain).

Iron and Steel

Iron is by far the most important structural metal. It is obtained by smelting iron ore with carbon, and the immediate product "invariably contains a certain amount of carbon." Wrought iron, steel, and cast iron are distinguished by their carbon content, and steels themselves may be characterized as low carbon (mild) or high carbon. Steels are further classified as carbon steels (just iron and carbon) or alloy steels (with additional alloying elements).

In 1631 Europe, wrought iron was the commercially dominant form. "Cast iron ... was not used much beyond pots, pans, cannon, cannon balls and bells" ("Iron," Boatright, *Grantville Gazette* III).

In April 1631, "single white iron" sold for 35 guilders per hundred pounds. The price subsequently rose, with a high of 48 in February 1634. Swedish iron was 6.92 in April 1631, dropped to 6.13 in February 1634, and peaked at 7.93 in March 1636. Steel in bars sold for 24.25 in April 1631, rose to 35.50 in May 1635, and then dropped to 27 in December 1636 (Posthumus).

In pre-Ring of Fire Europe, steel was made by the cementation method, "but it was difficult to impossible to make large forms like guns and cannon this way" (Boatright).

Canon is a little confusing as to the timing of subsequent advances. The White Diamond Steel Corporation manufactures steel by the crucible method beginning in 1632 (Mackey, *Essen Steel*, Chapter 2). I think in that year Jekli Koriska writes his partner Klaus that he is reconsidering investment in a steel puddling plant (the technique used to make steel in China). The letter implies that steel has not yet been made by the Bessemer or crucible methods ("Signs," Huff, *Grantville Gazette* 21).

In September 1634, Gary Reardon and Osker Geyer consider making steel by the Bessemer process (and the implication was that it hadn't been done yet) but decide that the puddling process better suits their needs ("SMC, Part 1," Watson, *Grantville Gazette* 71). Also in 1634, "Jacques [de Nonette] heard there was a research station somewhere else trying to get a Bessemer converter to work" ("Air France," Hare and Howard, *Grantville Gazette* 74), but it is possible that this was only addressing activities in France.

A plant is built in Linz that makes steel by the Bessemer process, but it blows up in September 1634, and in February 1635 it is being rebuilt (*1636: The Viennese Waltz*, Flint et al., Chapter 14).

But by whatever means, as of November 1635, "USE Steel is producing massive amounts, and now Sweden and Essen have increased their production as well" (*Bartley's Man*, Huff and Goodlett, Chapter 14).

There are numerous ferrous alloys but they will be discussed in the section on the corresponding alloying element (since that controls how soon it enters the timeline).

Copper

Copper is used both as the pure metal and in making alloys. Copper alloys include the brasses (zinc-copper alloys) and bronzes. The bronzes known to the down-timers are the tin bronzes; phosphor, aluminum, and silicon bronzes came later and will not be discussed in this section.

Copper is an excellent conductor of heat and electricity, and this has led to its use in heat exchangers and electric wiring, respectively. It is a strong enough structural metal to be used in roofing and plumbing, although bronze is stronger (hence its use in "elite" cannon despite its cost).

The metal is used in fittings inside hospitals and as copper sheathing for ships.. On the other hand, due to the toxicity of copper salts, it is disfavored for food processing (APV).

The price for Hamburg sheet copper was 53 guilders per hundred pounds in April 1631. During the period June 1631 to May 1637, there were several oscillations, with a high of 65 and a low of 47. Swedish gar-copper was 40 in June 1631, and subsequently experienced a high of 67.27 and low of 45. The earliest price I have for brass (wire) is 56, in 1669.

Silver

Silver was valued by the down-timers because of its rarity, shininess, and malleability. But it also has the highest thermal and electrical conductivity of the metals, and it has antibacterial activity.

I don't have a Posthumus price for "fine silver" in the 1630s. The earliest price I have for "fine silver" is 25.45 guilders per mark (July 1719). I believe the "mark" is about half a pound (the Cologne mark was 233.856 grams). At the same time, "fine gold in bars" was valued at 376.30 guilders per mark (Posthumus). That yields a gold/silver ratio of almost 15:1, which from a historic standpoint is rather high. The common metals mentioned in Posthumus were priced as follows: English tin (40 guilders per 100 pounds), English lead (6.3), Hamburg sheet copper (70), Norwegian gar-copper (68), Swedish garcopper (57), Spanish iron (7.25), Steermark steel (17).

The silver wage of unskilled workers in 1600-1649 averaged as follows: London (7.1 grams silver/day), Amsterdam (7.2), Paris (6.6), Madrid (8.0), Vienna (4.4), Leipzig (3.5), and Augsburg (4.0) (Broadberry).

Gold

Gold is soft and extremely malleable. It has high thermal and electrical conductivity and is a strong reflector of infrared radiation. It is also corro-sion-resistant. Prior to the Ring of Fire, it was used only in coinage, bullion, jewelry, and dentistry.

By 1559 ordinance, the Rhenish gulden of the Holy Roman Empire was 1/72nd of a Cologne mark of gold, 18.5 carats (77% pure), and thus 2.50 grams gold (Wikipedia). The Dutch guilder contained 0.856 grams fine gold in 1622 and 0.77 in 1638. It was considered equivalent to 10.28 grams silver in 1620-1659 (Garber note 2).

In 1623, the thirty-shilling British *rose ryal* had a fineness of 23.875/24 and a weight of 194.2 grams. With a mint indenture of 44 shillings per pound of gold, this yielded an implied official price of 3.727749 pounds per fine ounce. The implied official price for the twenty-shilling *unite* was similar (Officer).

In 1625, the gold-silver exchange ratio averaged 13:1 in Europe, 8:1 in China, and 13:1 in India. By 1650, it had increased to 14:1 in all three regions (Broadberry, but cp. 11-12:1 in Edvinsson 38).

Glass

The glass available before the Ring of Fire is soda lime glass, i.e., glass containing sodium and calcium as well as about 70% silica. Small amounts of other metal oxides may have been introduced to color the glass.

Glass's advantages are acid resistance (with exceptions), lightness, and (if decolorized) transparency; its disadvantages are brittleness and susceptibility to thermal shock.

Ceramic (Vitrified Clay)

"The word 'pottery' ... in its widest sense includes all objects fashioned from clay and then hardened by fire...." Glaze (a coating of fired glass) may be applied to the fired clay.

Traditional ceramics are made from clays or clayey shales, possibly with the addition of silica (as quartz sand, sandstone, or flint pebbles) and feldspar. The clay is shaped into bricks, pipes, or tiles, then heated (fired) in a kiln, resulting in partial vitrification of the silicate components of the clay.

Clay has been used to make pipes since Babylonian times, and the pipes at Ephesus are still functional. Clay has considerable compressive strength and is also abrasion resistant. However, it has low tensile strength, it is susceptible to thermal shock, and it has a high density, making it awkward to transport.

Stone

Stone construction materials include sedimentary (sandstone, limestone), igneous (granite, basalt, rhyolite, tuff), and metamorphic (marble, slate, soapstone, quartzite, gneiss) rocks, and laterite, which doesn't fit neatly into that classification. Stone cannot be cast or bent. It has to be broken into small enough pieces so it can be assembled into the desired shape. When stones are fitted together, binders are typically used to hold them in place. Binders include plaster and cement.

Wood

I discussed wood's use as a construction material in "The Wooden Wonders of Grantville" (*Grantville Gazette* 13).

Leather

Leather is an animal hide chemically treated to prevent deterioration. The characteristics of the leather depend on the type of hide, the tanning agent, and whether it is impregnated with any protective material.

Prior to the Ring of Fire, this was the preferred option for flexible, more or less air- and water-impermeable tubing. Leather was also used in the bellows of pumps.

Natural Fiber Textiles

We do not normally think of textiles as construction materials, but the down-timers use fabrics for sails, tents, and, with suitable waterproofing, flexible pipes. In the old timeline (OTL) they were used for the envelopes of balloons beginning in the late eighteenth century, and for airships and wings of airplanes, beginning in the nineteenth century. In pre-Ring of Fire Europe, the principal textiles are probably linen, cotton, wool, and silk.

Wood Tar

This is a polymeric coating material, typically derived from pine wood, and primarily used for waterproofing ropes, sails, and wooden hulls.

Graphite

Graphite is a crystalline form of carbon. Natural graphite was used prior to the Ring of Fire as a pigment and, in the case of the deposit in Borrowdale, England, as a refractory in cannonball molds. In 1634, Magda orders good English graphite ("wad") for use by the "telephone people" (*1634: The Galileo Affair*, Flint and Dennis, Chapter 29). There's reference to "graphite smuggling" in their *1635: A Parcel of Rogues*, Epilogue.

Canonized Up-Time Materials of Construction

Byproducts of Electrowinning

Many European mines exploited metal sulfide ores. Besides the metal that was of interest to the miners, these ores typically included other metals in varying amounts. Metal sulfide ore minerals include those of copper, silver, gold, zinc, cadmium, mercury, nickel, palladium, platinum, tin, lead, cobalt, iron, manganese, chromium, and molybdenum.

In August 1634, one Thuringian duke asks another rhetorically, "Do you have any idea how much copper, silver, nickel and cobalt we can produce from the hundreds of thousands Zentner of slag from the old smelts alone, when it's processed by electric power?" ("Ein Feste Burg, Episode 10," Prem, *Grantville Gazette* 49).

Electrochemical extraction is attractive in many situations, but it is not a panacea. In electrowinning, a metal-containing material (ore, slag, mine tailings) is dissolved in an aqueous electrolyte or a molten salt and subjected to an electric current in an electrolytic cell. Some metals are reduced and deposited on the cathode. Others are reduced, but sink to the bottom of the cell, forming an anodic sludge (slime). Still others remain in solution and must be extracted and reduced by chemical reactions.

The more positive the reduction potential of the metal, the easier it is to recover it by electrowinning (it "wants" to be elemental metal). The metals with a positive standard reduction potential are gold, platinum, palladium, mercury, silver, and copper. Of course, the amount of recovery of a given metal for a given electrical energy input depends on the concentration of the metal in the starting material and not just on the reduction potential. So, typically, a lot more copper is recovered than gold, even though gold has the higher potential.

Nickel has a slightly negative standard reduction potential (-0.23V). It can be recovered from the cathode, but only in a diaphragm cell that prevents the acid generated at the anode from redissolving the nickel deposited at the cathode. The pH and the nickel cation concentration in the solution must both be controlled. Note that if there are other metals present that are more electropositive than nickel, they will co-deposit with it. (Besides the metals mentioned previously, that would also include ferric iron, lead, and tin).

Alternatively, after electrowinning the more electropositive metals, nickel could be recovered from the electrolyte solution by chemical means.

The situation of cobalt (-0.28) is similar to that of nickel. Electrowinning of cadmium (-0.40), ferrous iron (-0.44), chromium (-0.74), and zinc (-0.76) is more difficult. That said, even aluminum (-1.67) is electrowon in the Hall-Heroult process.

The specific energy requirement (kWh/metric ton) is proportional to the total cell voltage (this includes the anode and cathode half-cell potential differences, resistance-related potential losses, and overpotentials) and the number of electrons moved per mole of metal, and inversely proportional to the atomic weight of the metal being reduced and the current efficiency (the percentage of the applied current that is actually participating in the reduction reaction). Some typical old timeline requirements for electrowinning were:

copper: 2,200 kWh/metric ton

zinc: 3,300

cobalt: 4,500

manganese: 8,000-9,000

aluminum: 13,000-15,000 (Hall-Heroult)

magnesium: 18,500

(Robinson).

If a metal has a reduction potential less than that of water (-0.83), as is the case for aluminum (-1.67) and magnesium (-2.38), then the process must be carried out in fused salt rather than aqueous electrolyte. This leads to increased energy costs for keeping the salt in the molten state. A suitable fused salt electrolyte must also be found, which was problematic for titanium.

In many electrowinning systems, gas is evolved at the anode. Oxygen may be safely vented into the atmosphere or captured for industrial use. If the gas in question is hydrogen (as in zinc electrowinning) or chlorine (as in magnesium electrowinning), the gas must be safely handled.

Electrorefining is a related process in which the metal of interest is refined by depositing it on the cathode of the electrolytic cell, the other metals remaining in solution. If these are of interest, they may be recovered by subsequent electrowinning or other processes. For electrical purposes, copper must be very pure and hence electrorefining of copper was commonplace in the late twentieth century.

The energy requirement for electrorefining is often less than 20% of that for electrowinning, as the required voltage is reduced, e.g., for copper, 0.15-0.3V vs. 2.2V (Robinson).

The terms electrorefining and electrowinning are used more or less interchangeably in Carroll and Wild, *Love and Chemistry* (Ring of Fire Press). In Spring 1635, Matthias notes that certain ore samples contained "more silver than I would have expected, a little gold, some other odds and ends," and comments, "not too hard to pull out, that's just electrochemistry." Raimund agrees, observing, "an electrorefining line doesn't seem all that complicated, if you could get us enough water power" (Chapter 6). There are further references to electrowinning in chapters 22 and 24. It appears that by January 1637, there is a "big shop" in Ilmenau doing electrowinning by the "older method" in which the sulfide ore is roasted before it is dissolved. And Matthias' company is an "electrolytic metal refining shop" selling "mostly copper and zinc."

Nickel and Nickel Alloys

By 1634, nickel has been found in tailings from more than one mine ("Sunday Driver," Runkle, *Grantville Gazette VI*). Presumably, these were German mines.

There is also nickel prospecting in the Sudbury, Ontario area in March 1635, and by May a mining site has been selected (*The Battle for Newfoundland*, Sakalaucks, Chapters 26-27). As of April 1635, there is a prospecting expedition to Kirkenes, Norway, looking for both nickel and iron. It is guided by a map with "resource markings" ("Catrin's Calling," Offord, *Grantville Gazette* 40). The *Hammond Citation World Atlas* has economic maps, and these show iron at Kirkenes and nickel at Petsamo (Pechenga) in modern Russia. The oversize National Geographic Atlas of the World also shows a Russian town near Kirkenes with the auspicious name of "Nikel."

A new, nickel-plated brass stethoscope makes an early 1636 appearance in "Gifts of Providence" (Howard and Carroll, *Grantville Gazette* 55). *Love and Chemistry* (Carroll and Wild, Chapter 22), set in Eisenach in August 1636, refers to sending hardware parts out for nickel plating.

While only nickel plating is specifically canonized, there is clearly the potential to make nickel-copper and nickel-iron alloys. Monel 400 is 66% nickel, 30% copper, 2% iron. Ni-resist cast iron is 3% carbon, with 13.5-36% nickel (Perry). In nickel bronzes, nickel replaces some of the tin (Brady 587). Dumet, an iron alloy with 42% nickel (Brady 519), is a low expansion metal suitable for junction to borosilicate glass.

There are a variety of fancy nickel alloys containing additional alloying elements, notably molybdenum (Hastelloy B-2 and Chlorimet 2) and chromium (Worthite), as well as one containing molybdenum, chromium, and tungsten (Hastelloy C-276), for which there is some promising corrosion resistance data in Perry and at least partial compositions in both Perry and Brady (586). But they are going to be pretty far down the timeline.

Aluminum and Aluminum Alloys

A large bauxite deposit is located in Suriname in February 1634 NTL ("Maria's Mission," Cooper, *1636: Seas of Fortune*). It is likely that a substantial quantity of bauxite made it back to Hamburg in September 1634. Some of that bauxite likely found its way into De Geer's hands ("Fire and Ice," Cooper, *Grantville Gazette* 35). Four pounds of bauxite makes two pounds of alumina, which in turn makes one pound of aluminum. The

Hall-Heroult process also needs a lot of electricity and cryolite as a flux. In 1635 NTL, De Geer sends an expedition to Greenland to mine cryolite ("Land of Ice and Sun," Mackey, *Grantville Gazette* 11).

However, De Geer runs into competition from the Danish crown, which at least nominally rules Greenland, and it (or a royal concession) takes over the mining of cryolite there. By 1636, the Surinamese bauxite is converted to alumina in Hamburg, and the alumina and cryolite are shipped to Glomfjord and Arendal, both in Norway, where hydroelectric power is being developed. HDG Laboratories has a research and development facility in Arendal where they are developing the techniques to smelt aluminum. Presumably from Arendal, Glomfjord receives "a few hundred kilograms of aluminum pipe" for use in "the nitric acid machines" ("A Trip to Glomfjord," Offord, *Grantville Gazette* 57). Bauxite is still being mined in Suriname in April-July 1636 ("Tears of the Sun, Milk of the Moon," Cooper, *1636: Seas of Fortune*). For more on the issues involved in obtaining aluminum, see "Aluminum: Will o' the Wisp," Cooper, *Grantville Gazette* 8.

It seems fairly likely that aluminum will be available, probably in "tens of tons" quantities, in 1637 or at the latest 1638.

Aluminum's advantages include high electrical and thermal conductivity, high reflectivity, high strength-to-weight ratio, low catalytic activity, ease of fabrication, and high corrosion resistance. However, the strength of pure aluminum and the 99%-plus alloys (1000 series) is lower than that of the other commercial alloys.

No aluminum alloy has been specifically mentioned by canon as available, but it is not unusual for people to refer to using "aluminum" when they are really using an aluminum alloy.

Use of aluminum alloys is much more common than that of the pure metal. In general, the alloys of aluminum with magnesium (5000 series), or with magnesium and silicon (6000 series), also have good corrosion resistance. The alloys of aluminum with zinc (7000 series) and even more so those with copper (2000) are usually much less resistant than pure aluminum to aqueous corrosion. Aluminum alloy plate has been protected by applying a thin layer of pure aluminum to both sides—"Alclad."

In those alloys, aluminum is the base metal. There are also alloys in which it is a minority component, such as aluminum brass and aluminum bronze.

Tungsten

Tungsten is important as an alloying element in steelmaking. The most economically significant ores are scheelite (calcium tungstate) and wolframite (iron manganese tungstate).

In canon, in 1632, Josh Modi tells de Geer that we can get tungsten "from the tailings of tin mines, according to the encyclopedias" ("Essen Steel, Part One: Crucibellus," Mackey, *Grantville Gazette* 7). That's correct. EB11/Wolframite says, "wolframite is commonly associated with tin-ores, as in many parts of Cornwall, Saxony and Bohemia."

"Wolframite" was coined in 1747 and is from German *wolf rahm*, "cream of the wolf." But the mineral was known before the Ring of Fire. Georg Bauer (Georgius Agricola), in *De Natura Fossilium*, wrote, "a certain black stone is found with a uniform color similar to the one from which tin is smelted but so light that one readily perceives that it is barren and contains no metal. We call this *spuma lupi*," meaning "froth of the wolf." It was called a "wolf" because it was thought to be devouring the tin.

It cannot actually be distinguished from cassiterite by its color, but cassiterite is harder than wolframite, and if we are lucky enough to find crystals, the forms are different. Chemical tests can distinguish them.

As EB11 notes, it is difficult to separate wolframite from cassiterite by gravity methods, as they are of nearly the same density. They can be separated magnetically, the wolframite being attracted. Since we don't have powerful rare earth magnets in the 1632 universe, we will probably need to use electromagnets, and that poses its own constraints, as generators and batteries must be developed and moved to the mining site (or the ore moved to them).

In September 1633, Don Francisco tells Mike Stearns that "the Chinese might be useful sources for zinc, graphite, mercury, antimony and tungsten," and that "the closer deposits are much smaller, subject to interdiction by our enemies, or both" (*1636: The China Venture*, Flint and Cooper, Prologue).

Don Francisco realized that while the wolframite deposits in Germany may be adequate for the next several years, they are considered minor by world standards, and a better source is needed in the long term. In World War I, Germany relied on stockpiled wolframite from Cornwall, and in World War II, on tungsten from Spain and Portugal. But in 1633 NTL, England and Spain (which controls Portugal) are hostile to the New United States.

EB11 and EB15 describe several different methods for smelting tungsten ore but ultimately the tungsten oxide is reduced with carbon under high heat.

Mining of wolframite is likely to be somewhat intermittent in the new timeline. The ceasefire in the Baltic War does not come until June 1634, and Saxony (where the tin mines are) is hostile and then war-torn until February 1636. My best guess is that tungsten will first be available in 1635 but production won't scale up until 1637 or 1638.

Cobalt

Prior to the Ring of Fire, the term "cobalt" (kobold or goblin ore) was a generic term for substances which, although resembling the desired metallic ore, were unproductive (EB11).The ores include cobaltite (cobalt sulfarsenide) and skutterudite (cobalt arsenide), and when roasted they produce toxic arsenical fumes. However, cobalt is usually obtained as a byproduct of nickel and copper mining.

Cobalt compounds have been used since ancient times to impart a blue color to glass and ceramics. The ancient Egyptian source was apparently a cobaltiferous alum.

In this article, cobalt is of interest as an alloying element. Kovar is a low-expansion iron alloy containing 28% nickel and 18% cobalt (Brady 519); it is a good match for borosilicate glass. (Some non-Grantville literature sources indicate that it also contains up to 0.2% chromium.)

Chromium and Stainless Steel

Chromium is used in two ways for corrosion control—the metal itself as chrome plating and as an alloying element to increase corrosion resistance. Notably, it is an essential ingredient of stainless steels and various tool steels.

Canonized, in this instance, doesn't mean available. Canon shows that an expedition was sent to Kemi, Finland, but not whether it was successful. Canon also shows interest in exploiting the serpentinite deposits in Maryland, but that was delayed, if not altogether frustrated, by the failure of the French to take immediate possession of the English colonies it purchased in North America.

Chromium makes possible other alloys beside stainless steels. One such is Worthite (24% nickel, 20% chromium), with sulfuric acid resistance superior to that of the stainless steels. Other alloys of interest contain molybdenum, and hence are discussed in the molybdenum section.

Plain and Reinforced Concrete

The making of plain concrete, common in Roman times, is almost a lost art as of the Ring of Fire, so I treat it as an up-time material. See "Better Foundations, Part 1: An Introduction to Concrete," Cooper, *Grantville Gazette* 19.

In 1632, Delia Higgins builds a warehouse with concrete pillars. She also becomes a patron of the Grantville High Tech Center's "brand new concrete research program" ("Other People's Money," Gorg Huff, *Grantville Gazette*, Volume 3). In "Second Starts" (Cooper, *1636: Seas of Fortune)*, there is a passing reference to a mysterious "concrete project" which is apparently looking for venture capital in July 1633. And in "Tears of the Sun, Milk of the Moon," the mooring tower for the airship is to have tripod supports fixed in concrete.

In 1634, the Duke of Sachsen-Eisenach is plainly interested in the possibility of using reinforced concrete for constructing a large cellar ("Ein Feste Burg, Episode 2," Prem, *Grantville Gazette* 41). However, I do not have a date for when reinforced concrete was first used in the 1632 universe.

As long as the concrete is intact, it serves to protect the steel reinforcement from the environment. The concrete is alkaline and a protective oxide layer forms on the steel. Chloride ions can be a problem as they disperse the oxide film.

Borosilicate Glass

Borosilicate glass is stronger, harder, and less susceptible to thermal shock than ordinary (soda lime) glass.

While borosilicate glass has not yet formally appeared in canon, borax and boric acid have. Borax (tincal) is already an article of commerce, imported from Tibet, as discussed in "Borax Bonanzas," Cooper, *Grantville Gazette* 28. In *1634: The Galileo Affair* (Flint and Dennis, Chapter 29), Sharon says that the Turks are the only ones who have it, but they are actually one of the many middlemen for borax. Although Turkey does have boracite, it was not discovered until 1865. Borax is used in a penicillin purification process in "The Prepared Mind" (Mackey, *Grantville Gazette* V).

In 1634, Lewis Bartolli goes to the Italies to look for boric acid in the Maremma of southern Tuscany. He gets a bit sidetracked by the Grand Duke's demand that he determine the authenticity of an artifact ("Under the Tuscan Son," Cooper, *Grantville Gazette* 9). Nonetheless, he presumably found it, because he uses boric acid in a chemical demonstration a bit later ("Arsenic and Old Italians," Cooper, *Grantville Gazette VII)*.

It is likely that the vacuum tubes mentioned in canon use borosilicate glass, to avoid thermal shock as the tubes heat up and cool down.

I previously discussed borosilicate glass in "In Vitro Veritas: Glassmaking After the Ring of Fire" (Cooper, *Grantville Gazette* 5).

Vulcanized Natural Rubber

While natural rubber was used in parts of Pre-Columbian America for various purposes, and in Mexico it was even vulcanized using the sulfur compound-containing juice of *Ipomea alba*, this did not excite much curiosity in Europe.

In the new timeline, rubber from *Hevea brasiliensis* is shipped from Brazil to Lisbon, beginning sometime in 1633 ("Amazon Adventure," Cooper, *1636: Seas of Fortune*). Also in 1633 (most likely in August), a French privateer captures one of the ships carrying this rubber and delivers it in Fall 1633 to Henri Beaubriand-Lévesque in Granville, France. Henri has studied Grantville literature and wishes to make vulcanized rubber (and use it for condoms). He succeeds by the winter of 1633-34 ("Letters from France," Offord, *Grantville Gazette* 12).

In July 1633, David de Vries sought investors for a colony in Suriname and hoped to find rubber trees (*Hevea guianensis*) there. ("Second Starts," Cooper, *id.*). The colony is established in February 1634, and De Vries leaves soon after. In May he is on the coast of Nicaragua, collecting rubber from *Castilla elastica* trees, which unfortunately were probably killed in the process of collection. This rubber is delivered to Hamburg in September 1634 ("Beyond the Line," Cooper, *id.*). I would assume it was vulcanized sometime in 1635.

In Europe, there is likely to have been some collection of milkweed rubber. ("Feng Shui for the Soul," Offord, *Grantville Gazette* 17). Milkweed is a bit problematic, because the rubber yield is low and there's a high resin content. For further information on natural rubber, see "Bouncing Back: Bringing Rubber to Grantville" (Cooper, *Grantville Gazette* 6).

Plastics

Balata, a natural plastic used for electrical insulation, was something that the colony in Suriname was expected to collect ("Maria's Mission," Cooper, *1636: Seas of Fortune*).

Primitive casein plastics have appeared in canon, as the result of treating milk with vinegar, a dilute solution of acetic acid ("Bootstrapping," Offord, *Grantville Gazette* 11); ("Songs and Ballads," DeMarce, *Grantville Gazette* 14). A related material (rennet-precipitated casein) actually predates the Ring of Fire. Alkali will dissolve both casseins. Primitive casein can be crosslinked with formaldehyde, making galalith, which is a bit more durable.

Bakelite (phenol-formaldehyde) is available in 1634 ("Feng Shui for the Soul," Offord, *Grantville Gazette VI*; *1636: The Chronicles of Dr. Gribbleflotz*, Offord and Boatright, Chapter 15). Bakelite is also mentioned as being available in small quantities in *1635: A Parcel of Rogues* (Flint and Dennis, Chapter 3)

By May, 1636, *Brennerei und Chemiefabrik Schwarza* manufactures gelatin silver-coated cellulose acetate and uses it to make sheet and roll film (*1636: The Chronicles of Dr. Gribbleflotz*, Offord and Boatright, Chapter 21). It may well have been made earlier, but it doesn't matter, as it is not really suitable as either a construction material or a corrosion-resistant coating.

Polyvinyl chloride (PVC) pipe is available by March 1637, but "there hasn't been much of it made yet and none of it is very good so far" (*1637: The Polish Maelstrom*, Flint, Chapter 30). There is reference to PVC in a greenhouse in Fall 1634 ("Botanical Liaisons," Palmer, *Grantville Gazette* 81), but I would assume that was repurposed up-time PVC. (I had predicted new PVC would first be made in 1635-37.)

I am not aware of any other synthetic plastics in canon.

Glass Fiber-Reinforced Plastics (GFRPs)

"Fiberglass," a rather unfortunate name for a glass fiber-reinforced plastic, is contemplated at least as early as December 1633 (*Bartley's Man*, Huff and Goodlett, Chapter 7). By 1634, some kind of fiberglass is used for an aircraft body ("The Boat," Offord, *Grantville Gazette* 30). One contemplated version was a composite of glass fibers and viscose, a cellulose derivative ("The Monster," Huff and Goodlett, *Grantville Gazette* 12).

Commander Cantrell's prosthetic is made using a mix of "fiberglass" and pine resin (*1636: Commander Cantrell in the West Indies*, Flint and Gannon, Chapter 1). I put "fiberglass" in quotes because here it no doubt simply means "glass fibers," but the prosthetic itself qualifies as a GFRP.

The preferred matrix material for fiberglass composites is actually an unsaturated polyester, and I predicted that it might be available in 1636-38 if made using fumaric acid isolated from natural sources. Vinyl ester and epoxy resins are also used as matrix materials, but I don't think they'll be available any earlier ("Industrial Alchemy, part 5: Polymers," Cooper, *Grantville Gazette* 29).

Coal and Coal Tar

Coal itself has been used as a fuel since the Bronze Age. Coal tar coatings date back at least to 1681 (Merten 1). A coal gas plant is in operation in Magdeburg in 1634 (*1634: The Baltic War*, Flint and Weber, chapter 2). This would produce not only coal gas, but also ammoniacal liquor, oils of various grades, coal tar, and coke. See "Industrial Alchemy, Part 4: Organic Chemical Feedstocks and Product Timeline," Cooper, *Grantville Gazette* 27.

Petroleum and Petroleum Tar

In areas where there are oil or tar seeps—for example, Baku—their use predates the Ring of Fire. They were used as medicines, fuels, military flammables, and waterproofing agents, depending on the time and location.

Wietze produces petroleum beginning in 1633 (*1633*, Flint and Weber, Chapter 11). The field was marked by the presence of oil seeps and tar pits ("The Oil Mines at Wietze and Pechelbronn," Corwith, *Grantville Gazette* 23). Petroleum tar may be mined from those pits. Additionally, the oil from the shallower layers at Wietze contain heavy oils which, after distillation, will leave a considerable amount of tarry residue.

Asphalt

This is probably a good time to mention that the term "tar" usually refers to the naturally occurring substance (whether of wood, coal, or petroleum derivation) and "bitumen" to the residue from petroleum distillation. Asphalt is a mixture of tar (or bitumen) with sand or gravel. Asphalt is made from Wietze bitumen in "Yes, Dear" (Howard and Copley, *Grantville Gazette VII*).

Impervious carbon is similar to asphalt, but it is graphite or bituminous coal particles bound by a resin.

Silicon Carbide

Silicon carbide, used as an abrasive as well as a refractory, may be made by fusing sand (silicon dioxide) and coke (Brady 792) at a temperature above 2204o C. Typically, an electric furnace is used.

"Your Tax Dollars at Work" (Offord, *Grantville Gazette* 68), set in February 1636, refers to a company named "Schubert's Abrasives." In its office there is a diagram of "the life cycle of silicon carbide and its uses," and the owner is observed "carefully sorting out silicon carbide crystals according to their size and color." (Pure silicon carbide is colorless; colors come from impurities, such as iron.) Canon does not state when the company was founded, and even if it did, that would not tell us when it first made or obtained silicon carbide. (It could have initially sold other, more readily available abrasives, such as sand, pumice, and emery.)

Uncanonized Future Materials of Construction

Manganese Alloys

Manganese is used as an alloying element. "Practically all commercial alloys of aluminum and magnesium contain manganese to improve corrosion resistance and mechanical properties" (EB15/Manganese). There are also manganese steels. In the form ferromanganese, it is used to remove oxygen and sulfur from carbon steel.

Manganese dioxide (pyrolusite) has been used since prehistoric times as a black pigment, but manganese is consigned to this section because elemental manganese was first produced in the 1770s. The pyrolusite may be reduced with carbon. At the end of the nineteenth century, pyrolusite was "extensively mined at Ilmenau and several other places in Thuringia..." and in 1893 a 97% pure manganese was prepared from pyrolusite (EB11).

In "The Kreutzer" (Grant, *Grantville Gazette* 94), Freeman says that "we" (meaning the up-timers?) have sources of manganese. It is unclear whether that means "know where it is" or "are already mining it." The story is set in 1635 (the 1622 one-kreutzer coin is thirteen years old).

Clear glass has been made in Europe prior to the Ring of Fire, indeed, as early as Roman times. The glass may be clear because it was made from low-iron silica, or because it contains a decolorizer (manganese or antimony oxide). The decolorizer might have already been present in the sand, or it might have been deliberately added by the glassmaker. There is, unfortunately, some debate about which of these explanations is correct (Jackson), but at some point, pyrolusite became known as "glassmakers' soap." If glassmakers were adding it deliberately, then they knew where to find it.

The principal barrier to exploitation of manganese is likely to be warfare and civil unrest in the areas where pyrolusite might be mined. However, Thuringia appears to be relatively free of conflict by 1633.

Synthetic Elastomers ("Rubbers")Is this the intended format?

I don't think any have appeared in canon yet. For predictions on availability, see "Industrial Alchemy, Part 5: Polymers," Cooper, Grantville Gazette 29.

Additional Carbon Derivatives

Both amorphous carbon (from bituminous coal) and graphite can be pulverized, compressed with a binder, and carbonized, forming carbon or graphite bricks. In the case of impervious carbon (graphite), the binder is a corrosion-resistant resin (Brady 149). Asphalts may also be combined with resins and rubbers.

Other Glasses

Aluminosilicate glass is at least alluded to in Grantville literature. I have found no reference to it in canon.

Fused silica (quartz) glass, 100% silica, is "the most heat resistant of all the glasses" and is also resistant to thermal shock. It has excellent chemical resistance. Unfortunately, it is costly and difficult to shape (Brady 408). The more common 96% silica glass has the properties one would expect.

The production of high silica glasses requires high-purity quartz (or other silica source) as a starting material, and a means for fusing the silica into a glass. The original fusion method was a hydrogen/oxygen flame, but it was superseded by an electric furnace.

Advanced Ceramics

Ceramics in general are composed of one or more oxides, nitrides, carbides, or borides, typically of silicon, aluminum, magnesium, calcium, or zirconium.

I have not found reference to any nitrides or borides in canon. Calcium carbide is mentioned in "Twenty-Eight Men" (Huston, *Grantville Gazette* 10), as a fuel for a miner's lamp. The carbide reacts with water to generate flammable acetylene. Because of its reaction with water, it is of no practical use as a ceramic.

Oxide ceramics. Silica of course is known to down-timers (as glass or sand), and kaolin is an aluminosilicate clay. Alumina (aluminum oxide) is obtained by processing of bauxite, a rather complex aluminum mineral. If aluminum is in canon, it may be presumed that alumina is, too.

Magnesia (magnesium oxide) may be made by baking magnesite (magnesium carbonate). Chromite is a mixture of iron and chromium oxide. Zirconia (zirconium oxide) may be found naturally as the mineral baddeleyite, but more often is obtained by treatment of zircon (zirconium silicate) in certain beach sands.

Silicon nitride may be produced by carbothermic reduction of sand (796). Tungsten carbide, used in drill bits, is trickier to make; a hydrocarbon vapor is reacted with tungsten at high temperature (924).

Glass-Ceramics

A glass-ceramic is a glass in which controlled crystallization has been induced. The crystallization is induced by a nucleating agent, and hence the kinds of glass-ceramics available will depend on which nucleating agents are known and available.

To make a glass-ceramic, "a standard glass formula, to which a nucleating agent such as titania has been added, is melted, rolled into sheet, and cooled. It is then heated to a temperature at which nucleation occurs" (CCD 417). The developmental bottleneck is likely to be the nucleating agent.

Silicon

Silicon is not a metal, but it is relevant in several respects. First, silicon is used as an alloying element, for example, in making silicon bronze, high-silicon cast iron, and a series of aluminum alloys. Second, silicon is used as a reducing agent in magnesium production. Third, silicon is needed to make silicone rubber (polysiloxane).

Once electric arc furnaces are available it should be possible to make silicon in fairly high purity by carbothermal reduction of quartzite or sand.

Silicon bronze is typically 96% copper. High-silicon cast irons have a silicon content of 13-16%.

Cadmium

Greenockite (cadmium sulfide) is associated with sphalerite (zinc sulfide), and cadmium is produced mainly from the flue-dust of zinc mining (EB 11/Cadmium)."Most cadmium produced is electroplated onto steel, iron, copper, brass, and other alloys to protect them from corrosion. Cadmium plating is especially resistant to attack by alkali" (EB15).

I do not think that cadmium will be used much for its corrosion re-sistance in the new timeline. Rather, it will be co-opted by the electrical industry for batteries and, as the sulfide, photoelectric cells. Or ignored altogether, because of its toxicity.

Platinum

Platinum was mined in Pre-Columbian America. I group it here because the Europeans didn't become interested in it until the late eighteenth century, and there's no reference in canon to anyone looking for it.

Palladium

Palladium is associated with platinum, gold, and silver. There are no refer-ences in canon to it, and its properties are similar to those of platinum.

Magnesium

Magnesium is the lightest structural metal, but the pure metal is not particularly strong. It is mainly used in alloys. There are alloys in which magnesium is the major component and others in which it is used to improve the properties of other metals (notably aluminum). Magnesium is also the key reducing agent in the production of titanium and zirconium.

Magnesium may be obtained from mixed chloride salts by melting the salt (magnesium chloride's melting point is $714°$ C, but the melting point of a mixed salt would depend on the constituents) and then subjecting it to electrolysis. Water must be excluded, and chlorine gas will be a byproduct.

The mixed chloride salts come from seawater or brine. They may be enriched for magnesium by differential solar evaporation, as magnesium (and calcium) chloride are less soluble than sodium or potassium chloride.

There are methods for separating the magnesium and calcium chlorides. One may add limewater (calcium hydroxide), thereby precipitating the magnesium as the hydroxide. You may then convert it back to the chloride with dilute hydrochloric acid, or heat it to drive off water and obtain magnesium oxide (see below).

An alternative source is magnesite (magnesium carbonate). It can be burned in the presence of coal to make the oxide (releasing carbon dioxide). Nowadays, China produces the majority of the world's magnesium metal by the Pidgeon process (silicothermic reduction of magnesium oxide). Carbothermic reduction is also possible with a high enough temperature.

Magnesium sulfate (Epsom salt) has appeared in canon as of February 1635 ("Birthing Pains, Part 2," Keener, *Grantville Gazette* 89). It was probably obtained by reacting a magnesium salt with sulfuric acid. However, it does occur in nature; e.g., in a bitter saline spring in Epsom, in Surrey,

England. The "bitter purging salts" were discovered in 1618 but not widely known in Europe until the early eighteenth century. In any event, the production of magnesium sulfate doesn't mean that we can make magnesium metal.

In *1636: The China Venture*, Chapter 26, Colonel von Siegroth mentions, "There was someone in Grantville who fired off some magnalium powder for my edification" (magnalium is a magnesium-aluminum alloy), and Eric Garlow says that he has some "magnesium ribbon...to show the Chinese scholars," but these may have been made prior to the Ring of Fire. Eric does know how magnesium metal was made, however.

Titanium and Titania

In canon, the Portuguese are collecting "black sand" in Kerala, India ("Gajam Raanni," Cooper, *Grantville Gazette* 25). These are heavy mineral deposits, and the Portuguese are most likely interested in the titanium ores rutile (titanium dioxide, titania) and ilmenite (titanium iron oxide).

Unfortunately, the processes for smelting titanium are, as Wikipedia puts it, "laborious and costly." The current commercial process (Kroll) relies on reduction of titanium tetrachloride with liquid magnesium (melting point 650° C) or sodium in an inert atmosphere of helium or argon (CCD 874). Or one can electrolyze titanium tetrachloride in a bath with fused alkali or alkaline earth chlorides (Id.). In our universe titanium is about six times as expensive as stainless steel.

I would not expect titanium to be available until a year or two after magnesium is first purified in quantity...whenever that might be. Titania is more accessible.

Zirconium and Zirconia

Zircon (zirconium silicate) is a component of beach sands in certain localities in Brazil, India, Australia, and Africa (Brady 995). I believe it is associated with the titanium minerals ilmenite and rutile. Zirconia (zirconium oxide) is a refractory ceramic.

Like titanium, zirconium is obtained by the Kroll process. That is, it is heated with carbon and chlorine to obtain the tetrachloride, which is then reduced with molten magnesium in an argon atmosphere.

Molybdenum

Molybdenum is an important steel-alloying element, imparting additional strength and corrosion resistance. It is also found in some nickel alloys.

The principal ore is molybdenite (molybdenum disulfide). In canon, by September 1635, Osker Geyer has accessed some limited source of molybdenum ("SMC, Part 3," Watson, *Grantville Gazette* 73). It is just enough for five special pistols, and even then Geyer had to compromise on the formula for ordnance steel. He doesn't name his source, but my best guess is that some molybdenite specimens were found in tin mine tailings from the Saxon Erzgebirge. But Germany was not an economically viable source of molybdenite up-time, and the tin-molybdenum association is not a strong one.

There is also a partial association between tungsten and molybdenum. A secondary tungsten ore, wulfenite, is lead molybdate, and may be found in association with molybdenite.

This is alluded to in *1636: The China Venture*, Flint and Cooper, Chapter 53. Xu Xiake had looked for wolframite (iron manganese tungstate) in the vicinity of Dayu. He can't help but also collect any rock that looks interesting, and he gives Eva Huber what he thinks is graphite-and-quartz. The "graphite," however, passes the "acid test" for molybdenite.

Wolframite was mined in Saxony, at a site located between Pechtelsgrün and Stangengrün, in 1934-1969, and molybdenite was also found there (Mindat). However, this wolframite site does not appear in Grantville literature, so I think it an unlikely source.

The logical place to look for molybdenite is in southern Norway, as indicated in *Hammond Citation World Atlas*. The mapped locality is certainly the Knaben molybdenum mine. Mining began at the outcrop "Blyantberget" (the pencil rock) in 1885-1887 (Mindat). Molybdenite, a soft mineral, was easily confused with the graphite used in pencils, and both were confused with lead. The Knaben mine was active during both world wars.

The molybdenite is roasted, converting it into the trioxide. EB11 says that this can be reduced by heating it with carbon in an electric furnace or by the Goldschmidt method. (This is code for aluminothermic reduction.) EB15 instead refers to reduction with hydrogen. Both descriptions skip over purification steps. For the purpose of steelmaking, you don't need the pure metal, just the purified molybdenum trioxide, although it is more common to add molybdenum in the form of ferromolybdenum. The latter is made by mixing the pure molybdenum oxide with iron oxide and reducing the mixture with aluminum (thermite reaction).

All of this points to molybdenum being a relatively easy to obtain alloying element, but canon suggests that molybdenite is first available in quantity in 1636 or later, and there may be dramatic reasons for the editors to further delay the advent of molybdenum steel.

The Knaben ore actually averages only 0.2% molybdenite, although there are pockets of nearly pure molybdenite (RockandGem). So that perhaps gives us an excuse for postponing molybdenum development, if an excuse is needed. Considerable machinery would be needed for concentration.

Niobium and Tantalum

Niobium (columbium) is used in ferritic stainless steels to inhibit intergranular corrosion (EB15). It is very difficult to separate it from tantalum.

Tantalum is used, like tungsten, in crucibles for separation of molten rare earth elements (EB15/rare-earth-element).

The principal ore of tantalum is tantalite (CCD 846), a variety of columbite. Essentially, columbite has variable proportions of iron, manganese, tantalum, and niobium. It is known to be found "in some abundance in the deposits of cassiterite in the tin-field of Greenbushes in the Blackwood district, Western Australia" (EB11/Columbite). It is also found in Madagascar and South Dakota (EB15/Tantalite), in Nigeria (associated with tin), and in Kinshasa, Congo (EB15/Niobium Processing).

Pyrochlore is a niobium ore found in Minas Gerais and Goiás, Brazil, and St. Honoré, Quebec (EB15/Niobium Processing). The latter is not far from Quebec City.

The processing of the ores depends very much on the elemental composition but the reduction of the metal is typically aluminothermic.

I find it difficult to believe that niobium or columbium will be available in the new timeline 1630s.

Iridium and Osmium

Iridium "dissolves in mineral acids but is unaffected by potassium hydroxide or boiling water. When heated in the presence of the halogens or sulfur, direct combination takes place" (EB11; EB15). Small amounts of iridium are commonly added to platinum, particularly for surgical pins (EB15/Platinum).

Osmium "in the massive state...is insoluble in all acids, but when freshly precipitated from solutions it dissolves in fuming nitric acid. On fusion with caustic potash it yields potassium osmate. It combines with fluorine at 100° C, and when heated with chlorine it forms a mixture of chlorides" (EB11).

Iridosmine is an alloy of iridium and osmium that occurs in gold-bearing conglomerates and gold sands. "Because of their hardness and resistance to corrosion, both natural and synthetic iridosmine are used for tips of pen nibs, surgical needles, and sparking points in engines" (EB15).

Iridium and osmium are both byproducts of platinum mining and refining.

Conclusion

Both old and new materials of construction will serve as building blocks for the industries of the new timeline.

Bibliography

George S. Brady, Henry R. Clauser, John A. Vaccari. *Materials Handbook*. 14th edition. McGraw-Hill, 1996.

Stephen Broadberry, Bishnupriya Gupta. "Monetary and Real Aspects of the Great Divergence Between Europe and Asia, 1500-1800."

Rodney Edvinsson, Tor Jacobson, Daniel Waldenström. "Exchange Rates, Prices, and Wages, 1277-2008."

John Emsley. *Nature's Building Blocks: An A-Z Guide to the Elements.* 2nd edition. Oxford University Press, 2011.

EB11 and EB15 refer to the eleventh and fifteenth editions, respectively, of Encyclopedia Britannica.

Michael Free et al. "Electrometallurgy—Now and in the Future." 2012. https://www.researchgate.net/publication/267802677_Electrometall urgy_-_Now_and_in_the_Future

Paul Garber. *Famous First Bubbles: The Fundamentals of Early Manias.* MIT Press, 2001.

Anna K. Hodgkinson et al. "The Use of Cobalt in 18th Dynasty Blue Glass from Amarna: the results from an on-site analysis using portable XRF technology." *STAR: Science and Technology of Archaeological Research,* August 12, 2019.

Carolyn Jackson. "Making Colourless Glass in the Roman Period." *Archaeometry,* 47(4): 763-780 (2005).

Lawrence A. Officer. "What Was the Price of Gold Then? A Data Study." University of Illinois at Chicago, no date.

Van Osnabruggue. "Money in the 17th century Netherlands." 2016.

Robinson. "Electrochemical Processing." In Eckroth, *Encyclopedia of Chemical Technology.* 3d edition. Volume 8. 1978.

Steve Voynick. "Rock Science: The Knaben Molybdenite Mines." *Rock&Gem,* April 2, 2020.

Acknowledgements

T hank you to our proofreaders! They are responsible for a definite step up in the quality of stories, articles, and columns.

Paul Goodspeed

Janet Lewis

Helen Monath

Mark Pottenger

Tim Sayeau

Paul Standring

Everyone who is writing in 1632/Ring of Fire, Time Spike, and Alexander Inheritance. As a reminder, we can accept works of up to 17,500 words. To those of you who continue working on books even though there are no guarantees: Bravo!

Everyone who has bought issues and subscriptions of *Eric Flint's 1632 & Beyond*. Thank you so much!

New Books
Available Now & Coming Soon

Flint's Shards, Inc.

Available Now

A Diogenes Club for the Czar
Gorg Huff and Paula Goodlett

This is the fourth Miroslava Holmes book and all the Holmes books have dealt with Russian politics, but this one deals with them even more. Events from *1638: The Sovereign States* are included in this novel and from there it continues the main Russian thread of the 1632 Universe.

Czar Mikhail Romanov of the United Sovereign States of Russia has problems by the score.

The Embassy Bureau is run by an incompetent from an important family, who is possibly a traitor. Sheremetev is gone, only to be replaced by Mikhail's Uncle Ivan, who, if he's as corrupt as Sheremetev was, is a lot more competent. The advances in technology mean that while Mikhail can defend himself against Muscovite Russia, he doesn't have the forces to defeat it.

So, it's looking like a long, stalemated war.

Russia can't afford a long war. Every Sovereign States port is blocked by Muscovite Russia or Sweden. Even if Mikhail should defeat Muscovite Russia, the Polish-Lithuanian Commonwealth would still be sitting between him and western Europe. His foreign credit is failing and the conflict between the free states and the serf states is getting ready to shatter his new nation before the ink is dry on his new constitution. The royal chef can't prepare a proper croissant. The Pravdivye Fakty is printing fantasies and code groups that are telling the Muscovites who his agents are, while the only private detective in Russia is off on the far end of Kazakh.

Now someone has killed a congressman.

What's a czar to do? Mikhail needs another Grantville. Another Ring of Fire to bring innovations to Russia, enough innovations so that the rich and powerful can't steal all the new wealth before it reaches the poor.

Mikhail doesn't ask for it but he gets what he needs. Because what he needs is A Diogenes Club for the Czar.

* * *

Coming Soon

An Angel Called Peterbilt
Eric Flint, Gorg Huff, and Paula Goodlett

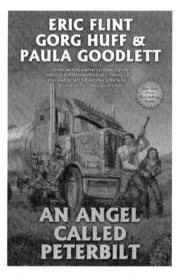

HISTORY WILL NEVER BE THE SAME AFTER A PETERBILT TANKER TRUCK FULL OF OIL IS TRANS-PORTED BACK ONE THOUSAND YEARS IN TIME. A NEW NOVEL IN ERIC FLINT'S ASSITI SHARDS SERIES BY RING-OF-FIRE STALWARTS GORG HUFF AND PAULA GOODLETT.

Michael and Melanie Anderle are hauling a tanker full of oil with their Peterbilt eighteen-wheeler when they're struck by a temporal irregularity that sends them, the truck, and their daughter back in time a thousand years. The bubble that transports them also grabs a chemist and her two young children, along with half a convenience store in the middle of the United States.

They just want to make a decent life for themselves in this new world of the past, with their Peterbilt and its oil providing a means of transportation, a generator, and shelter. But not all the locals are willing to live and let live, and when the area shamans decide that this community of temporally displaced persons is a threat to their power, the Anderles find out what it's like to take a Peterbilt to war.

It is currently in the Baen February 2024 bundle here:

https://www.baen.com/w202402-february-2024-monthly-baen-bundle.html

It will be available February 6, 2024 here:

https://www.baen.com/an-angel-called-peterbilt.html

***

Missions of Security
Bjorn Hasseler

Neustatter's European Security Services is open for business, and business is . . . *too* good?

With the National Guard, private industry, and even a seemingly tranquil farming village caught in an explosive political crossroads all relying on NESS for missions of security, Neustatter and Astrid find themselves pressed to staff, train, and equip the agency while keeping up with their clients' growing requirements in scope and complexity.

-- A simple railway escort mission involves a secretive manufacturing client from Grantville bearing mysterious cargo and a captured fugitive all destined for Magdeburg during the Baltic War . . . what could possibly go wrong?

-- The Bible Society hires NESS to guard a flock of Anabaptist, Catholic, and Lutheran high schoolers *en route* to riot-torn Erfurt and Jena, but will NESS's own pastor tear them apart first?

-- Already strapped for personnel, the last thing Neustatter needs is for a regiment of dragoon militia to choose their wagon train for . . .

"involuntary provisioning." Can a handful of badly outnumbered agents protect a village that isn't sure it wants their help?

Missions of Security is the sequel to *A Matter of Security*, and contains the full text of the previously published short story, "Blood in Erfurt."

It is currently in the Baen February 2024 bundle here:

https://www.baen.com/w202402-february-2024-monthly-baen-bundl e.html

It will be available February 6, 2024 here:

https://www.baen.com/missions-of-security.html

***

Security Threats
Bjorn Hasseler

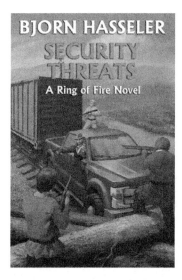

Neustatter's European Security Services encounters a campaign of industrial sabotage, a pastor who attempts to limit their client base, an espionage ring, and the aftermath of the Dreeson assassination. Old nemeses and new allies complicate matters.

Somewhere in Grantville is a missing heiress. There's also a Resistance, and it has cookies. Even repeat business with established clients is complicated, not to mention dangerous. Real life proves more complicated than Neustatter's movies or Astrid's books as NESS looks for common threads. Which incidents are related and which are not?

For Astrid Schäubin, solving cases, directing operations, and even portraying a saint are one thing, but figuring out dating in the midst of everything that's happening is quite another.

Security Threats is the third book in the NESS series, after *A Matter of Security* and *Missions of Security*.

It is currently in the Baen March 2024 bundle here:

https://www.baen.com/w202403-march-2024-monthly-baen-bundle.html

It will be available March 5, 2024 here:

https://www.baen.com/security-threats.html

Connect with Eric Flint's 1632 & Beyond

We would love to hear from you here at *Eric Flint's 1632 & Beyond!* There are lots of ways to get in touch with us and we look forward to hearing from you.

Main Sites

Email: 1632Magazine@1632Magazine.com

Shop: 1632Magazine.com

Author Site: Author.1632Magazine.com

For anyone interested in writing in the 1632verse, or fans interested in more background on the series and how we keep track of everything.

Social Media

Our Facebook Group is our primary social media, but we do use the FB Page, YouTube, and Instagram accounts.

Facebook Group: The Grantville Gazette / 1632 & Beyond

YouTube: 1632andBeyond

Facebook Page: Facebook.com/t1632andBeyond

Reviews and More

Because reviews really do matter, especially for small publishers and indie authors, please take a few minutes to post a review online or wherever you find books, and don't forget to tell your friends to check us out!

You are welcome to join us on **BaensBar.net**. Most of the chatting about 1632 on the Bar is in the 1632 Tech forum. If you want to read and comment on possible future stories, check out 1632 Slush (stories) and 1632 Slush Comments on BaensBar.net.

If you are interested in writing in the 1632 universe, that's fabulous! Please visit **Author.1632Magazine.com** (QR code above) for more information.

Printed in Great Britain
by Amazon

49308387R00099